Jasmine!

Thanks for your continued support!! :)

Marena

Rose City Ink Presents…

Written By,

Marina J

&

Shelli Marie

Printed in the USA

Publisher: Rose City Ink

Editor/Proofreader: Shelli Marie/Marina J

ACKNOWLEDGEMENTS
(Marina J)

I first want to give a major shout out to Ms. Shelli Marie for collaborating with me on this project. You have always been an inspiration to me and it's been an honor to be able to work with you.

As always I have to thank my team ZitrO Publications. Divine and Nkki Ortiz you guys are the best! This year we're going to rock the literary world….they ain't ready. Lol.

To my girls Jerrona and Rachel, we've been through the fire and we've come out unscathed. That just goes to show you that not even the devil could deter us. I love you guys.

Let me not forget my babies, the Super Six. Mommy loves you guys and everything I do, I do it for you all.

To all the readers who continue to support me, it is very, very much appreciated and I will continue to thank each and every one of y'all every chance I get. I now turn things over to my wonderful co-writer.

Thanks for supporting Marina J!

ACKNOWLEDGEMENTS

(Shelli Marie)

To God Almighty I give the glory!

To my family support team:
Anthony, Jeremy, Jessica, Danielle, and Vassie Jr.
Thanks for all of your encouragement.
I love you guys! Always!!

To the rest of the Dishman Klan:
Jennifer Dishman, Kim Dishman,
Marlo and Devin Dishman
Daddy and Genora Dishman
I love you all dearly!!

To Marina J, I thank you with all my heart to ask me to do this book with you. I am very honored and truly had a ball writing it, especially knowing that this story means a lot to you. I wish you nothing but the best Chica!! Nothing but LOVE!! Always Sis!!

To my extended support team: Special Thanks to Sheila James, Teruka B, TonYelle Reese-Britt, Alexys Price, JeaNida Luckie-Weatherall, and Lakeisha Holmes, thanks for the encouragement and also for always showing me LOVE!!

Thanks for supporting Shelli Marie

DEDICATIONS
(MARINA J)

Even though this is an embellishment of our story, it's our story nonetheless. I dedicate this to you, my wonderful, loving and always supportive husband. I love you Timothy.

DEDICATIONS
(SHELLI MARIE)

Marina J, this is for you Sis!! Thanks for allowing me to help you share your amazing story! For that I'm grateful...

Nothing but LOVE... Always

Marina

"I hope my momma didn't hear ya loud ass mouth Colay!" I whispered as I slipped my nightgown back on.

"I'm tired of climbin' out this damn window," he complained as he pulled me near and kissed me one last time. "Ya lucky I love ya ass. I'll see ya at school tomorrow."

Standing in the window, I watched Colay jump from the top of the awning down to the grass. He looked up at me and waved before he ran off.

Going to the kitchen to get something to drink, I assumed everyone in the house was sleep at one in the morning. Boy was my ass wrong.

"You aint gonna be fuckin' all up in my house little girl!" my mother spat as she crept up behind me.

"Dang, that was rude," I mumbled.

"No, what's rude is you fuckin' up in my house!"

I rolled my eyes and huffed as I carried my tail right back to my room to avoid further confrontations. After slamming my door so I could ignore her bitching, I slid on my earphones and listened to some music.

With me being caught up in love at an early age, nobody could tell me shit. My life revolved around Colay Smith. He was not only a handsome chocolate hunk of a young man he also was able to win me over with his kindness. After learning I was knocked up during our senior year, he had convinced me to marry him as soon as we graduated high school.

Once in his grip, my dreams of going to college were a thing of the past. Colay had something entirely different planned for me. He wanted me barefoot and pregnant. His controlling ass kept me that way for the next nine years, during which I birthed six beautiful children. I wouldn't trade them for the world. They were the only reason I survived the physical and mental abuse placed upon me by their father. I was determined to give them a better life.

"Mommy, you are so beautiful," my oldest daughter complimented as she brushed my hair. "Why do you let daddy hit you like that and mark up your face? If I were you, I would clock him upside the head and make him leave!"

My heart dropped at the hurtful words that escaped my baby's lips. She was so innocent and Colay had always spoiled her, so I was quite surprised at her outburst.

"Your daddy loves you baby," I assured her with a smile.

"Yeah, I know he does, but that's not enough," she replied with a serious expression. "He needs to love and respect you too mommy."

That was it. There was no way in hell that I could ignore my daughters' feelings. To be so young and capable of understanding something so complex was unbelievable.

"So, what are you gonna do mommy?" she inquired before leaving the room.

"I'm not gonna let it happen again baby," I promised. "If it does I will take all of you and leave."

Running to give me a big hug, she held on to me for dear life. I didn't question her. I just squeezed her until she was ready to release me.

The very next morning, I dropped the older kids off at school and the younger ones off at the sitter's. I had to go downtown to take care of some business. I needed to file for divorce and that's just what I did. I didn't wait for the next fight. Instead I avoided it at all costs.

Remaining on my best behavior for the next six months, I was able to stack my money in order to get an apartment for me and my kids once I left Colay. Working an office job at a grocery store wasn't cutting it. Even though I graduated at the top of my class in high school and took a few hybrid courses, I couldn't get a good job without a damn college degree.

When the time came for me to leave my husband as well as Chicago, I was going to be ready. There was no way that I could remain in the same state with him and expect to have any type of peace. I had to move somewhere far away.

Having no one to talk to, I turned to my boss, Mrs. Swanson. After spilling my guts to her about what I had been going through, she offered to help by presenting me with a position at one of our chain stores in North Carolina.

Mrs. Swanson felt so bad for me that she not only gave me a promotion, she paid for my entire trip there. She also set me up at an extended stay for a month until I was able to find a place to live. That was all I needed to make my move. I was set.

Waiting until late one night when my husband was passed out from an all-night drinking binge with his boys, I quietly rounded up my children and strapped them in the van one by one. I already had my trailer packed and hitched to the back so as soon as I clicked my own seatbelt, we were off.

Taking thirteen hours to arrive, I made it there in the early afternoon on a Saturday. I went to my spot and checked in. That's when I met this young girl named Cheryl. Even though she was only twenty, she had the ambition of a responsible adult. Every word that she spoke pertained to making money or saving it. She had the hook up with just about everything from boosters to fake EBT cards.

"I need to find an apartment," I confessed to Cheryl before I left to drop my children off.

My previous boss had graciously paid for them to go to a summer camp that was for all ages. She anticipated that I would need the time to search for a place for me and my children.

"When you're done taking the kids, meet me here," she suggested as she handed me the address to a complex that was nearby. "We have four bedrooms and they're really affordable."

"Thanks Cheryl. I'll be there within the hour."

While rushing to get there, I began to worry about filling out an application. I had absolutely no rental history so I was unsure if my paperwork would be accepted. I told Cheryl my problem and she assured me that she would speak to the landlord for me.

While filling out the necessary documents, Cheryl went to the back office and closed the door. She was only in there for a few minutes before she came out smiling. I had not a clue what she said to him, but he came out moments later with my keys. I paid my deposit and went to get my things.

"I told ya girl," she laughed. "Here's my number. Call me when you pull up and I'll have my man Terrell and his friend's help you bring everything in."

"Are you sure," I questioned hesitantly. "You have done more than enough for me already."

"That's what we're supposed to do girl!" she spat with a big grin. "That's why the world is so fucked up today. Don't nobody ever want to help the next person unless it's something in it for them! My reward I'm gonna collect in heaven!"

As much as Cheryl cursed, I knew she couldn't be a church goer, but her beliefs and good deeds led me to trust she was Christian at heart. That was good enough for me because I definitely didn't need any fake ass bitches in my circle.

Everything went according to plan and by eight I had all my things in the apartment and my kids in the bed. That gave me and Cheryl time to talk. She started the conversation by asking me why I moved. Holding nothing back, I released the gruesome details about my failed marriage.

"I'm so damn glad you left that fool Marina!" she admitted as she helped me rearrange my sofa and chairs. "You think he's gonna come up here actin' a fool?"

"I have a temporary order of protection and they already served it to him. I don't think he'll risk his precious freedom to come and find me," I replied with a twinge of fear. "And if that motherfucker has enough sense, he will remember that I'm licensed to carry a gun."

I wasn't certain if I had enough nerve to ever shoot my soon to be ex-husband but what I did know was that I had enough dirt on him to get his ass in a world of trouble in the streets. In the past, I had always been so scared of him but not anymore. His threats and fists could hurt me no longer.

"Since your kids are already in the bed, why don't you come over and watch 'No Good Deeds'?" she suggested. "I just got it on bootleg girl!"

I had wanted to see that flick for a minute but hadn't gotten a chance because of everything that had been going on. Plus, it was damn near impossible to get a babysitter after hours.

"Sure, let me take a shower right quick. All this movin' got me sweaty and shit," I responded before walking her to the door. "Give me about twenty minutes."

After bathing, I put on an oversized T-shirt and some cut off denim shorts. My hair was messy and I didn't feel like fucking with it so I slicked it up into a loose bun on the top of my head.

Before leaving out, I went and kissed every last one of my precious children. Then I turned on the baby monitor, snatched up the handset and shoved it in my purse so that I could hear if the kids woke up. It had a pretty good reception range so I was certain that it would work at Cheryl's apartment which was right next door.

"Just in time," she laughed as she ushered me in and handed me a bowl of hot buttered popcorn and a Coke.

Scanning the front room, I noticed an unfamiliar face.

"I didn't know you had company," I smiled feeling a little bashful.

"Oh yeah, that's right," Cheryl laughed. "You didn't meet my man's brother Timothy earlier. Yeah, he missed out on the heavy work."

Timothy quickly got up and shook my hand. He was quite handsome, but he looked rather young. With me being twenty six, I knew I had to have him by at least five years.

"Would you like something to drink?" he offered.

"Are you old enough to be drinking?" I teased.

Everyone began to laugh at him until he pulled his identification card out and flashed it.

"Oh, y'all quiet now huh?" he taunted. "I can't believe y'all clownin' like that knowin' good and damn well can't none of y'all go and buy ya own damn alcohol by ya self except for Cheryl."

That shut every last one of them the fuck up. I was a little impressed.

"Sure, you can pour me a small glass," I replied with a flirtatious smile.

Yes, Timothy was young, but it was something about him that screamed 'Great Catch'. I knew better than to rush into anything, but I was definitely interested to find out more about this handsome fella.

Once the movie ended, Timothy offered to walk me out. I was a little tipsy, but I allowed it.

"I appreciate you makin' sure I got in safely," I thanked him and shook his hand. "You seem like a good dude and I could use a *friend* in my life right now."

Timothy left that night without saying too much, but I saw him damn near every day after that and things began to shift in a positive direction. He made it a point to come and check on me and my kids and for that I was grateful. How could I not fall for him?

Timothy

I wasn't the average nigga. I never got emotional over a female. Besides my mama and grandma, I never met a chick who could get me to give them my heart until I met Marina. She was older than me by five years. I wanted to approach her but I thought to myself, what could I possibly have to offer her?

I was twenty one years old, still living with my mama and I didn't have a job. What woman would want a broke nigga? I didn't want to take the chance of approaching her and she rejected me. The only way I was going to do that was if I had my shit together. I couldn't just step to her and expect her to take care of me. Naw I was a man about my shit. I wanted to be able to give her whatever it was that she needed because she was one of those types of women. By that I mean that she was amazing! She always handled her business no matter what. I wanted to lighten her load for her. I wanted to love her. I wanted her to be mine and only mine. I was on a mission.

When I met Marina she was living next door to my brother Terrell's girlfriend. She was always at work. I rarely saw her but when I did, I made it my business to talk to her. We always had conversations about any and everything. She was really intelligent. I loved chopping it up with her. I noticed a lot of dudes in the neighborhood trying to talk to her but each time she would shut them down. I laughed on the outside but on the inside I was jealous as hell. I hadn't directly come out and staked my claim but niggas should've known because I was always around her.

Marina told me one time that I was the only man she had allowed in her home. I felt special about that. To think that all those niggas around there stayed in her face all the time and none of them had even had action at entering her house.

Marina had six children; three girls and three boys. I admired her and how she took care of her kids because I had five siblings myself so I knew the struggle. I often wondered if she ever got tired. It had to take a lot out of a person to take care of a big family, work a job and do it all alone.

Over time I learned that Marina was originally from Chicago and her divorce was about to be final. She was always taking care of everybody else. She was the one who needed taking care of and I was just that person. I was just waiting for the perfect opportunity to approach her. I was really feeling her. Maybe more than any other female I had ever been with. Something told me that she was the one but

I wanted to know for sure. I didn't have to wait too long to find that out.

"Yay! Woo hoo! I is FREE!" Marina yelled hopping out her van. I was sitting on the steps to Cheryl's apartment when she pulled up and hopped out. She seemed really cheerful and I was glad. It wasn't often that I had seen Marina happy but for some reason, that day she was overly excited. I knew eventually she would come tell me why, but at the moment I just basked in her joy.

Marina spoke to me as she ran inside Cheryl's house. She was waving some papers around and yelling out about how good it was to finally be free. I took it that whatever it was, she was going to be celebrating later.

That night was going to be the night. I was going to step to her and let her know I had been feeling her for a while now. Right then though, I just wanted to be happy for whatever it was that she was free from.

Marina was sitting over in her house with a few of her girlfriends and a couple bottles. Apparently her divorce was finalized. I could see why she was happy.

My brother kept trying to get me to go over to her house to get him a cup of Bacardi but I didn't want to.

Marina wouldn't give him a drink because he was underage. He knew she was sweet on me so that's why he sent me over there. I couldn't lie. I wanted to go celebrate with her anyway but I wasn't a drinker. I needed an excuse to go over to her house, so I did what my brother asked me to do.

I loved seeing the smile on her face and it did something to me. I caught myself falling for her and didn't even know it.

Knock-knock!

Marina's door was open but I wasn't a rude nigga. I didn't just walk up in folks houses like that. Marina looked up at me with glassy eyes and the widest smile ever.

"Hey boo what's up?"

"Hey. I just wanted to know if I could drink with you."

"Now you know damn well you ain't a drinker!"

"Yeah well tonight I am."

I saw the look of surprise flash across her face but she obliged my request.

"Nigga you know where I keep everything so get your own drink. I ain't making it for you."

I walked into her house and towards the kitchen. I know what you're thinking. She was a little rude just there right? Wrong! That's just the way she talked to everybody. It didn't bother me not one bit though. In fact, it kind of turned me on.

As I was pouring myself a drink I heard somebody behind me. It was Marina. This was it. I had to make my move. As I was thinking about how to say something to her, she came on to me.

"How much of my drink you taking?"

I lifted my cup up to show her.

"So what you gone give me for that drink?"

I could tell she was slightly intoxicated but I didn't care. In fact, I played along with her. I reached into my pockets and saw her shaking her head. I gave her a puzzled look and when she noticed, she spoke again.

"I don't want what's in your pockets fool!"

"Well what you want then?"

Suddenly, Marina walked all up into my personal space. She was close enough for me to smell the light scent of her body spray. It was something fruity but it smelled good as hell. She looked me dead in my eye before she pulled me to her and pressed her lips against mine. It was a slow, deep, sensual type of kiss, the kind that instantly got my dick hard. I didn't expect that shit! I was shocked though because I had never had a woman come on to me like she was doing. She broke our kiss, looked at me and said.....

"You staying with me tonight. So do whatever you gotta do now, but make sure you bring yo ass back to me."

"You got it. I ain't going nowhere."

After all Marina's friends left it was half past nine. Her kids had been in bed for well over an hour already so I knew they were asleep. Me, Terrell, his girl Cheryl and a few others we knew were all sitting out on the porch when Marina came to her door and told me to come on. Actually her exact words were, "If you coming then bring ya ass on!"

I had to admire that about her. She wasn't afraid to speak what was on her mind or say anything she felt like saying. Everybody looked shocked when I hopped my ass up off the porch to go inside Marina's house.

When I went in, she locked the door behind me. I barely got to turn around when she had me pinned up against the wall with her tongue down my throat once again. I felt my dick begin to rise. I didn't know what the hell that woman was doing to me but I was enjoying the hell out of it. Don't get me wrong, I had girlfriends before but in order for my dick to get hard I had to either stroke it myself or get them to give me head. Marina didn't even have to do shit but kiss me. Now that was a bad bitch right there.

I knew that I was going to enjoy being with her. My only worry was if I could give her what she needed. I would soon find out if I could or not.

Marina

The day I got my divorce papers, I didn't know how to act. I was running around screaming and hollering. That was my first day of freedom and I was opened to date anyone I wanted. I already had someone in mind.

"Let's have a celebration at my house Cheryl!" I proposed.

"Yeah, now that I'm twenty one, I'll bring the drinks!"

"But ya man aint," I teased. "So no bottom-ups for his ass over here."

I was stern about serving alcohol to minors. I wasn't with it. What they did in their own house was on them, but up in my crib it wasn't happening.

"Be over here by seven," I requested as I ran off to get things ready.

Now I hadn't been much of a drinker, but that night I let loose and had one too many. The more I stared over at Timothy, the more I knew I wanted him in the worst way.

Knowing that he had no idea I was feeling him in that manner, I chose to ease up on the situation and tread lightly. I didn't want to scare him off by being aggressive. It had been a minute since I had a nice stiff one and I was craving that shit.

Soon as the opportunity arose, I jumped on it and invited him back inside once everyone was gone. The minute he came in my door all that playing the shy girl role went out the damn window.

That was the first night Timothy and I made love. Age didn't have shit to do with what he threw on me that night. He had my ass begging for more.

"As much as I would love to stay here and wake up in your arms, I have to respect your kids," Timothy admitted as he clinched my palm.

Being the kind of guy he was, he led me to the shower in my private bathroom and we both climbed in. As he washed my back, he revealed his true feelings.

"Damn, I hate to admit the shit, but I knew I had to have you the moment I saw ya ass."

"Really?" I giggled as he rinsed the soap off of me.

"Hell yeah girl!" Timothy whispered in my ear.

My breasts were tickled as he brushed across them with the bath sponge. I was getting horny all over again.

Turning me towards him, he confessed that he wanted to take our relationship to the next level. I was hesitant, but definitely open to the idea. But, I did have a few concerns.

"So Timothy," I spoke as I dried my body. "Do you think you could be with a woman that has a ready-made family?"

"If you're referring to your kids, I know that you guys are a package deal," he explained. "If I love a woman, I love her for her entirety."

Timothy kissed my lips to hush me up from responding.

"Now think about that when you go to sleep," he requested before disappearing out of the door.

Seven o'clock came too damn quickly for my taste; especially to be woke the hell up by laughing and yelling. My kids never slept in. They were always up by the crack of dawn. They knew to wash their face and brush their teeth before breathing up in anyone's damn face with some dragon breath. It was a daily routine and I was proud of them for sticking to it without being constantly reminded.

"Mommy, someone's knocking," my oldest daughter yelled through my closed bedroom door. "It's Tim! Can we let him in?"

Before I could answer her, I heard his voice. It wasn't anybody but my oldest son that opened the damn door, with his greedy ass.

"He brought us some breakfast mommy!"

"Say what?" I thought to myself as I rushed to freshen up and fix my bedhead.

"Good Morning Beautiful," Timothy greeted me with a kiss to the cheek as he served my children who were sitting at the table.

Every last one of them began to laugh and coo. Even my littlest one raised his hands and shook in his highchair as he slopped eggs all over the place.

"Mommy your face is turning red," my daughter teased. "That means your blushing!"

I waved them off and led Timothy into the living room to ensure a little privacy.

"You know you really didn't have to do all this," I expressed with a bashful smile.

"I know that Marina," he flirted with a tilted head and ran his tongue across his lower lip.

Damn, that shit turned me the fuck on…

"I did it because I wanted to," he confessed. "You do things like this for the people you care about. Is that alright with you?"

It damn sure was and I was going to be certain to make him know that shit a little later.

"Come back at noon and maybe I can return the favor," I suggested.

Timothy kind of looked at me funny, so I questioned his expression.

"It's just that I'm not used to seeing this side of you," he confessed.

"Whatcha mean by that?"

"Well, you're usually so hard and shit. You know with that slick ass tongue of yours."

"Is that a bad thing?"

"Hell the fuck naw," Timothy laughed. "That shit is sexy like a motherfucker. *'Hard on the streets and soft in the sheets'*. That's what's up."

I couldn't help but to laugh at the way he put that shit because that was me to a fucking 'T'.

"I'll be here," he promised and sealed it with a quick kiss before the kids could catch us.

It was Saturday and Cheryl had already volunteered to take the children to the park for a few hours. She had to use my van in order to transport all of them, but I was cool with that.

I couldn't get them cleaned up and dressed fast enough. Lucky for me that I was always organized. I had to keep shit in order. That was the only way I could smoothly run a household single handedly. It wasn't anything new to me. Hell, I had been doing that shit even when I was married to Colay.

"Are the kids ready?" Cheryl inquired the moment she saw me step out front to get some fresh air.

"Hell yeah, are you?"

"Toss me the keys and help me get them in and we're up out this bitch!" she replied. "I packed us some lunches and snacks too so we'll be straight."

She hadn't said nothing but a motherfucking word. I ran in the house and rounded them up. We got that shit done so fast that they were screeching off ten minutes later.

And fifteen minutes after that, Timothy was at my door...

Timothy

I caught myself spending so much time at Marina's house that I barely saw my mama. I made it a point to go check on her since she only lived up the block. That day though, I was helping Marina get ready for her son's birthday party. He was turning five. She went all out for little man too! She had everything a kid could ask for when it came to a birthday party.

Since it was the end of August she decided to have a barbecue for him. My brother and I were getting the grill ready as Marina and Cheryl prepared the sides. Those women definitely knew how to throw down in the kitchen. They were making potato salad, Spanish rice, beef and beans, mac and cheese. The list went on and on. All the kids were out back running around and playing while the ladies were inside each of their kitchens.

Marina hollered out for me to go get the door because somebody was knocking. Well beating on the door was more like it. I snatched it open ready to go the fuck off when some dude just pushed his way past me.

"Who the fuck are you and where is my wife?"

It was none other than the infamous Colay. I stared that nigga down with so much venom he had to feel that shit. I knew of his past with Marina and I wanted to beat his ass for what he did to her. She sat up many of nights telling me how that asshole had mentally and physically abused her. I guess his ass didn't know shit about how to treat a woman. *Well this down south, country born and bred nigga was about to show his ass what to do with a woman like her.*

"Marina! It's for you."

"Babe who is-"

Marina looked like she saw a ghost when she noticed who it was. All the color drained from her face and she started shaking uncontrollably. I could tell she was scared so I went to my woman.

Her ex-husband must have really done a number on her for her to be that scared. I could see the tears in her eyes getting ready to drop so I stepped up.

"Check it out homeboy. I respect who you are but you ain't gonna be busting up in my girl's house like this."

"Nigga sit yo country ass the fuck down somewhere! This is between me and my wife!"

"Ex-wife homeboy. She's your ex-wife. Now I'm only gonna say this shit once. Back yo ass up off my woman and leave."

That nigga had the fucking nerve to stand there laughing at me. I wanted to knock his ass out for that but Marina stepped in between us and spoke up.

"Look Colay, you know good and damned well we're divorced. If you want to speak with or see your children they're in the back, but if not then you need to leave my house."

"Oh bitch you got a backbone now? What? This nigga done pumped ya head up or somethin'? You know you ain't shit and I own ya ass. I guess imma have to show because you done forgot."

Colay raised his hand to hit Marina and that's when I snatched his ass up. I didn't know who that nigga thought he was but I was about to show him how down south niggas did.

We ended up in a full on tussle in Marina's living room. I could hear Marina screaming for me to stop but I was in the zone. I repeatedly punched Colay in his face over and over again. That's when I felt a pair of strong hands grab me. I was about to go ham when I realized it was Terrell. Stepping away from that nigga, I left his ass lying on the floor in the fetal position.

"He don't have all that mouth now," I thought to myself.

What I did didn't really set in until one of the kids ran in and saw their father on the floor all busted up. They immediately burst into tears.

"Daddy? Is that my daddy?"

Marina turned quickly to usher the kids back outside. I felt bad for Lupe seeing her father like that. I didn't expect for shit to go that far but Colay left me no choice. I had to defend what was mine and that was my woman. Ain't no way in hell I was gonna let him come up in her house and beat her ass. If there was one thing I didn't tolerate, it was a man putting his hands on a woman. My father never did that shit so I was taught never to do it. Apparently Colay never got the fucking lesson. *Well hopefully he learned now.*

Terrell and I picked Colay's sorry ass up off the floor and started ushering him to the door when Marina came back in. Her face was red, she'd been crying and she was clearly pissed off. She looked at me with appreciation but when she turned to Colay, there was fire in her eyes.

"How dare you just pop up at my home, tryin' to start some shit and then turn into a little bitch when you get your ass whooped. Doesn't feel good does it?"

Colay just looked at Marina with hatred. I knew then it wouldn't be the last time we saw his ass. I was more than ready though. I was gonna defend my woman at all costs.

The rest of the day went off without a hitch. I had even sat down and talked with Lupe, apologizing to her about what she saw. She understood and that shocked me seeing as she was only six years old. She told me it was about time somebody did to him what he did to her mommy. That hurt my soul to know that these precious little babies knew more than they should have for their ages. I made a vow right then and there that I would protect them from everything or die trying.

Marina

After Colay showed up at my door I thought I was going to die. If it wasn't for Timothy, I think I may have.

I was so happy that my kids didn't see their daddy get his ass handed to him the way he did. Hell, I was embarrassed for him.

Timothy calmed down as soon as everyone came in, but me on the other hand, was hotter than fish grease. I was able to contain my anger until after the children were asleep.

"What the fuck was I supposed to do with this, throw it at him?" I ranted as I held up my order of protection and waved it around in the air.

"Marina, sit down and relax baby," Timothy urged as he helped me come out of my clothes. "Imma run you a nice hot bath, light some candles and let you have some peace and quiet while I straighten up in the front."

That's just what I needed at the moment and I was grateful to have Timothy there to help me out.

"Damn, it feels so fuckin' great for someone to have my back for a change," I thought to myself as I submerged my body down into the hot bubbly water.

Closing my eyes, I allowed my mind to drift on a way to keep Colay at a distance. I started to send him a text message and just tell his ass, but before I could do that, my cell began to ring.

Reaching for a towel, I dried my hands and connected the call.

"Marina you must have lost ya fuckin' mind to think you could up and move and take my damn kids!" Colay yelled into the phone. "And ya dude must be an even bigger fool to think that he can get away with the shit he pulled today. This shit is far from over!"

"Look Colay, I don't know how you got my digits, but lose the shit! Ya comin' over here and callin' me clearly violates this restraining order I have against you! This is plenty enough to get ya ass locked the fuck up for a pretty minute or two!"

All the hollering and screaming must have alerted Timothy because within seconds he was busting through the bathroom door. The expression of rage that displayed across his face insisted for me to let him handle it.

Stepping to me, Timothy snatched the phone from my ear and began to verbally assassinate Colay.

"Look bro, get ya shit together! Ya lost the little scuffle and ya lost ya woman. Now I would never stand in the way of you seein' ya seeds but they are my responsibility now. This is my family!" he barked. "The sooner you chalk ya loss up to the game, the sooner ya ass can move the fuck on! Now, if you haven't had enough nigga just try me!"

There was a pause in the conversation before Timothy pressed 'end' on the screen and powered the phone off. He then set it on the counter, handed me a towel and helped me out the tub.

"We gonna have to teach this motherfucker a street lesson. A lesson on life before that nigga loses his!"

"What did he say babe?" I inquired as I slid into my panties and shirt.

"He told me to watch my fuckin' back!" Timothy snapped as we walked into the bedroom. "I don't take too kindly to threats! I hope that nigga don't try no funny shit!"

"Let's not worry about all that right now," I suggested as I pulled back the sheets and patted his spot. "Right now I need a stress reliever. You got that for me baby?"

Laying back onto my pillow, I spread my legs and motioned for him to come to me. Within seconds, Timothy was undressed and had his tongue all up in my candy stash.

"Damn baby," I moaned as I reached my peak the first time.

Hitting all my sensitive spots, Timothy pleased me until I couldn't go anymore. He was the one usually tapping out, but that night it was me.

"You alright babe?"

"I am now," I whispered as I snuggled into his chest and began to doze off.

I had never in my life felt so safe and secure. I had absolutely no complaints. I was right where I wanted to be.

The following morning was Sunday. That was supposed to be my day to relax and do nothing. The kids were up getting ready to go to an excursion with the children's church. The van was coming to pick them up soon.

"I'm gonna walk the kids outside to wait for their ride," Timothy yelled out.

I could hear all my babies screaming goodbye and telling me they loved me before the door slammed. I turned over in the bed and buried my face into the pillow.

About twenty minutes into my doze, I heard several gunshots. Jumping up in a panic, not realizing that I was dressed only in my T-shirt and panties, I darted outside to see what had happened.

"Lord please let my babies be alright," I prayed silently as I watched everyone screaming and running around in a panic.

As I neared the sidewalk, I just about passed out. It was Timothy. He was sprawled out on the ground in a small pool of blood. No one was helping him!

"What the fuck happened?" I yelled as I held my man's head in my lap. "Someone call a fuckin' ambulance!"

Allowing my emotions to get the best of me, I cried hysterically.

"Help me!" I continued to holler out to no one in particular. "Help me!"

"Where's the kids?" Cheryl questioned as she rushed up to me and dialed for emergency assistance. "Is Tim okay?"

"The kids are already gone," I explained through my tears. "I don't know what happened. I just ran out here when I heard the gunshots."

Cheryl's hands were trembling so bad that she could barely clinch her cell. I hurried to take it from her so I could tell them where we were.

"We already have an ambulance on the way," the operator informed me. "Is the victim conscious?"

"No, but I feel him breathing," I sniffled.

Hearing the sirens get louder let me know that help was near.

"Hold on Tim," I begged. "Don't you dare die on me!"

His eyes opened briefly and then rolled back to the back of his head.

"Please stand back ma'am," the paramedic demanded. "He's going into shock. We have to get him stabilized before we get him in the back!"

Standing out of the way, I held on to Cheryl and continued to weep. I could barely keep still or control my body from trembling.

"Okay, he's good. Let's go," he yelled out as they lifted the stretcher onto the ambulance. "You can ride with us to the hospital if you like."

Cheryl told me to go ahead. She promised to be there to pick the kids up when the van dropped them back off as she handed me a pair of sweats and my slippers. I hugged her, thanked her, and then hurried to get strapped in.

Holding on to Timothy's hand, I squeezed it tightly and continued to pray for him. There was no way I could bare to see my man in the state he was in, let alone die…

Timothy

I had just finished putting the kids on the church van when I heard a screech of tires. I looked to my left and an all-black Acura was headed my way. At first I thought it was Colay trying to jump me but instead that nigga pulled a strap out and began blasting. I couldn't believe his bitch ass shot me! I felt the first bullet enter my stomach and I fell from the pain. On the way down he shot me again in the shoulder then skeeted off. I hoped somebody heard that shit and I didn't die out there on Marina's doorstep.

There were sirens and I heard Marina and Cheryl saying something but everything sounded so far away. I felt myself getting ready to drift away when several strong hands started working on me. I was glad because I wasn't ready to go yet. I needed to be there for my family and my woman. I was going to try my best to get through this.

They loaded me into the ambulance and we rode off. I could hear Marina by my side mumbling to God to please bring me through this. I wished I could say something to her but I was void of speaking.

We arrived at Cape Fear Valley Medical Center in no time. I was going in and out of consciousness. I heard them yelling out my stats as they wheeled me in. A doctor yelled for them to get me to the O.R. immediately. I didn't want Marina to think I didn't know she was there so I mustered up all the energy that I had left and clutched her palm.

"He squeezed my hand!" She screamed.

That was the last thing I heard before I passed out.

When I came to, I had no idea how long I had been out of it. It was a beautiful thing to open my eyes and see my woman right there by my side. Terrell, Cheryl and even my mama was there. I stirred in the bed and that alarmed Marina.

"Baby can you hear me?"

"Yeah babe. What the fuck happened?"

"You were shot. Do you know who did it?"

"Yeah it was your bitch ass baby daddy. When I catch that nigga, he's dead!"

I meant what I said too. I knew that he was the father of her kids but to shoot me was the ultimate no-no. How does a nigga get that mad over an ass whooping he asked for and come back to shoot a nigga? That was some pussy shit if you ask me. Yeah, as soon as I caught that nigga it was on and popping. There was nothing nobody could tell me or stop me from doing it. It wasn't like we had some real beef between us. He was just mad that I had Marina. That was exactly what I meant about niggas getting all up in their feelings when a female didn't want them. Colay was definitely in that position.

After a while, a doctor came in to check me out and updated my progress. He let me know that I had been shot in the stomach and right shoulder but luckily no vital organs or veins were hit. I was expected to make a full recovery but I would be out of commission for at least four to six weeks. I wasn't mad though because that gave me just enough time to come up with a plot to get that nigga back. I wanted to have a full proof plan in place for when it all went down because I didn't need anything to lead back to me.

Not too long after the doctor made his exit, the boys in blue made their entrance. I didn't want to talk to no pigs so I was very vague with my answers. They asked if I knew who shot me and all of that but I told them I didn't remember shit.

One of the detectives kept staring at me like he could see straight through my bullshit, but I still wasn't telling them a damn thing. They could ask me as many questions as they wanted but they would still get the same answer over and over again. I was gonna handle the shit in the streets. The same way he brought it to me, I was going to bring it to him.

They kept me in the hospital for about a week before they discharged me. I was glad to be going home. I wanted to take a hot bath, eat some good food and lay up with my woman. I wanted some pussy too but I couldn't do too much so I was out of luck.

Just because I couldn't freak my woman like I wanted to didn't mean I couldn't please her. I was gonna show her that night. She stood by my side the entire time I was in the hospital and still managed to handle her business. That was a real ass woman.

Marina got me back to her house and wouldn't let me do shit. She ran a bath for me and even washed a nigga down. She paid extra special attention to my dick. I couldn't lie, that shit felt really good the way she was stroking me. I hadn't been able to dive in that good pussy since I had been shot. Knowing it would be a few more weeks before I could, I sat back and enjoyed that shit. She helped me out the tub and dried me off before leading me to her bedroom.

I was feeling good, courtesy of my baby. What I didn't know was that she was about to make me feel great. When we got in her room she closed the door and locked it. I gave her a puzzled look when she snatched my towel from around my waist. She dropped to her knees and started stroking my semi-hard dick. Before she could say anything I felt her wet mouth on my shaft. I let out a low groan. She was bobbing her head up and down while stroking it at the same time. I couldn't resist. I grabbed a hand full of her hair. I just had to.

I busted a nut in no time. I knew baby girl had skills but I didn't know it was like that.

Now I'm a nigga and I got plenty head before, but that shit right there topped the cake. I ain't never had my toes curl, my legs go weak and feel that shit from head to toe ever in my life. Marina was the truth! I was glad she was mine though. She was definitely a down ass bitch. I knew I would hurt her by killing her baby daddy but shit it was either him or me. There was no way I could let him continue to walk the streets after what he did.

At least she knew and if she had a problem with what I planned on doing then she kept it to herself. I felt like I would be doing her and the kids a favor in the long run because if his scary ass could shoot me, then he could and probably would do the same to them.

Marina was a broken yet beautiful woman. Her kids were just as much a joy to be around as when I was hanging with their mom. There was no way I would let shit happen to any of them. All I had was time to come up with the perfect plan. I hoped his mama had a black dress because in a few short weeks, it was definitely about to be some slow singing and flower bringing round those parts. For now, time was his best friend.

Marina

After discovering that Colay was behind the shooting, I had to find a way to talk to him. I knew Timothy was going to have an issue with it so I had to figure out how to do it without letting him know. He was spending the night at his mother's house who had been really worried about him.

"Momma, daddy at the door," my oldest daughter hollered out. "Do you want us to let him in or naw?"

So much for calling Colay. He beat me to it by showing up unannounced at my house.

"Naw, let me get that shit," I yelled back as I headed to the door. "Y'all go to your rooms while I handle this."

The younger kids began to pout but my oldest wasn't having it. She hurried to escort each of them to their rooms like a good big sister.

"What the fuck you want?" I snapped. "You gotta a lot of fuckin' nerves showin' up over here after you shot Tim!"

"I don't know what the hell ya talkin' about Marina," Colay straight lied to my damn face. "I just came to see my kids."

"There's no way you're coming in my house, so wait ya ass right the fuck here while I get them."

After closing the door and locking it, I rushed to my room to pull out my order of protection and dialed the non-emergency police.

"My ex-husband is over here threatening me and I have a restraining order against him," I pretended to cry. "I'm scared to death and he won't leave!"

"We have a unit in your area ma'am. Stay in the house and the officer will identify himself when he arrives."

She wanted to stay on the phone with me, but I lied and told her my battery was about to die. She bought my story and within minutes I could hear a commotion on the other side of my door.

"Is daddy still here?" my daughter inquired as she poked her head out of her room. "No, he's gone baby but don't come out just yet."

She winked, smiled and closed herself back in with her siblings. Soon as she was out of sight, I crept to the door and eased it open.

"Seriously ya snitch ass bitch!" Colay yelled. "Ya really called the law on a nigga behind some raggedy ass fool you got around my kids and shit!"

One of the officers asked to see my paperwork, once satisfied, they hauled his ass right on downtown. I knew it wouldn't do much, but it bought me some time to think of another way to get back at him for shooting Timothy.

Things stayed calm in my house for several hours after that. The kids kept quiet and played in their rooms, except for my oldest who had to come and check on me.

"Momma don't worry," Mariela urged. "You are the strongest woman I know! Tim will protect us. He will be back soon and he won't let daddy hurt you ever again!"

"That's my girl," I laughed. "You always know how to make me smile."

We hugged and went in the kitchen to make dinner. She insisted on making burgers. She pulled the George Foreman grill out and told me that she wanted to do everything.

"You go sit down and relax momma," she insisted. "I got this."

My daughter had done it a few times before with my help, but I was sure she had it. I retreated to my room to get some rest.

Even though Timothy had only been gone since that morning, I missed him already. I really needed to see him.

Calling up Cheryl, I asked her to keep an eye on the kids while I went to see my man.

"I'll bathe them and send them to bed first," I assured her.

"Girl please," Cheryl laughed. "If you left right now, they would be fine. That daughter of yours got shit in order and the rest know what to do. Hell, I never have a problem with them. They're all a bunch of sweethearts."

"Awww thanks so much Cheryl," I acknowledged. "I'm gonna leave out in about an hour. I'll call you when I'm ready."

By the time I got changed, the kids had already eaten, cleaned and were now getting their pajama's on. I peeked into their rooms and called them all over to give me kisses. My baby boy was the first one to me. He clung onto my leg so tight that he almost made me fall over.

"Mommy, can you read to me?"

"Of course baby."

All my babies gathered around while he ran off and got his favorite book, Dr. Seuss's Green Eggs and Ham. I read it to them, kissed them again and was out the door.

"Hey Marina," Terrell yelled the moment I stepped out of my place. "Are you going over to my mom's?"

"Yeah, is Cheryl ready to come and sit with the kids?"

"She's coming," he laughed. "She had to go back in and get her damn book."

"What is that girl reading now?"

"Something called 'Loving my Husband & Yours Too'!" he huffed. "What kind of shit is that? I don't need her to get no ideas!"

"Shut the hell up!" Cheryl clowned as she locked her front door. "This book right here is the shit! You don't know nothin' bout all this!"

"You betta not know nothin' bout that shit either!" he teased with a pinch to her ass.

"Cut that shit out!" Cheryl giggled. "Wait until I read my next book on the list, 'No Bitch in my Blood'! You really won't wanna fuck with me after that one!"

Terrell laughed his girl off and waiting for her to go into my house before he began to run down a plan he had to get back at Colay for shooting my man. It was kind of farfetched so I came at him with an alternate angle.

"Well I have a lot of connections back in Chicago."

I explained how my ex-husband was involved in some illegal activities back home. Colay had a legitimate job but he continued to slang dope on the side. He had stolen money from Amon who was the kingpin in the hood I grew up in. After he did it, he blamed it on his best friend Troy.

"Word?"

"Yeah, and the bad part about it was they murked his homeboy."

"Let's go see how Tim is doing and fill him in on all this shit," he suggested.

We hopped in separate rides and headed to see the man who now held my heart...

Timothy

I heard a few car doors slam so I peeked out the window. I saw that it was only Marina and Terrell approaching the front door so I relaxed a little. I listened as they both spoke to mama before climbing the stairs. I was anxious to get in the streets so I could catch Colay's sorry ass but between my mama and Marina, that was hard to do.

When my brother and my woman finally walked into my bedroom I could tell they were up to something. I looked back and forth between them trying to figure out just what that was. I knew it had to be serious though because the expressions on their faces gave them away.

"Hey babe. How you feeling?"

"I'm good babe but what's going on? I can tell that you and Terrell been talking bout something."

"Actually we were and we were coming up with a plan to get back at Colay's bitch ass without getting our hands dirty."

"Yeah bruh. Marina done told me some shit about that nigga that's beneficial to us. If we do this shit just right, we won't have to worry about a muthafuckin' thang!"

"Ok then. Tell me what's up."

I listened to Marina run down the story about how Colay used to run drugs for a dude named Amon back in Chicago. Apparently he stole money from this dude and that was going to be our way to get revenge.

Marina had made a few calls back home and come to find out, there was a quarter million dollar street bounty out on Colay.

Word in Chicago was that Colay set Troy up but after Troy was killed, the truth came out. Troy felt like Colay was gonna be a snake so he recorded a conversation between him and Colay one day where he was bragging about stealing Amon's money. Colay didn't know shit about the recording and Troy damn sure wasn't going to tell him. Long story short, Troy gave the recording to his sister and told her that if anything happened to him, give it to Amon.

By the time Amon got word that it was Colay who stole the money from him and not Troy, he was long gone to North Carolina to find Marina and the kids.

Shit just got real!

Not only could I get rid of that nigga, I could also make some serious money in the process. That would most definitely come in handy. I could use that to take care of Marina and the kids for the rest of our lives.

We all sat around planning on how we were gonna get Colay back for shooting me and get the money in the process. Terrell said he didn't even want any of the ends. He just wanted that nigga dead. Marina and I still decided to give him fifty thousand for helping us out.

The plan was to send Marina back to Chicago to talk to Amon while Terrell kept tabs on Colay's every move. When I was well enough, it would be my job to snatch Colay's ass up and deliver him to Amon. I was confident that our plan would work.

Terrell left and it was just me and my baby. I so badly wanted to give Marina the business but I still wasn't able to. However, there was one thing I could do.

Marina looked at me with a devilish grin. I knew she was on the same page as me right then. I crept over to close and lock my door. When I turned back around she was lying across the bed looking all sexy. I pulled her to edge of the bed and kissed her hard. She greedily sucked my bottom lip. That shit turned me the fuck on and my dick immediately rose to the occasion, as usual. I gently pushed her down on the bed before reaching to remove her leggings. When I slid them down I realized she wasn't wearing any panties. That worked for me.

I dove face first into her sticky wet treasure box. She smelled so good and tasted even better. I couldn't get enough of her. I licked and slurped her second set of lips like it was the last thing I would ever taste. I could hear her trying to control her moans but that shit was so sexy to me. It only made me go harder. I felt her legs clench up and her breathing got real shallow. I knew my baby was about to cum, and I was going to catch every drop.

Marina busted a nut and begged me to stop but I didn't listen to her. I kept going letting her bust two more times before I released her. Her juices covered my face but I didn't care. Shit her nectar could cover anything it wanted right about then. Just the thought of her sliding down my pole got my dick harder than it already was.

Since she hadn't moved, I took my chances. While she lay there with her eyes closed, I dropped my draws and slid right up in that. She was shocked but a low moan escaped her lips when I was fully entered. I knew I wasn't supposed to be straining myself but I couldn't help it. I needed some of her good loving.

"Babe are you sure you want to do this? You're not even healed yet."

"I know babe but if I go one more day without feeling you, I'm gonna explode!"

Marina didn't say anything else after that. She allowed me to stroke her down with no objections. I made sweet love to my woman for the next hour before I was totally exhausted.

Afterwards she helped me wash up and got me back in the bed. I was already on the way to sleep when I whispered to Marina, "I love you babe."

Marina

When I got to Timothy's mom's house, I called back home to Chicago to find out what I could. I had brought the trouble into our relationship, so it was only right that I did my part to get it removed.

First I dialed up my homegirl Shandy. She fucked around with Colay's brother. She told me that Colay hadn't been seen around town in weeks and that she heard he was staying with one of his cousins in North Carolina. What a damn coincidence.

"Can you find out where his cousin lives and text me the address?"

"Hell yeah! I hope Colay gets everything he got comin' to his trifling tail," she spat.

"Me too!"

"I heard you got his ass locked up," she inquired.

"Yeah, but a lot of good that did! They let his ass right the fuck out!"

Briefly explaining the incident, I had her gasping. I didn't reveal too much, only the parts I wanted her to relay. She definitely had a big fucking mouth.

After hanging up with Shandy, I dialed Colay's homeboy Brown. He and my ex were on again, off again, friends. I was hoping to catch him in his hating stage.

"What's up Marina?"

"Hey Brown, I was just callin' to catch up on the happenings out there."

"Naw, ya ass is calling about Colay!"

"Aight, what if I am?"

"Then stay ya ass away from him! All I'm gonna say is, Amon got a quarter million dollar death wish on that nigga! I hate to see you and ya kids get caught up in the crossfire."

That was enough info for me. That shit had my head spinning. Timothy must have sensed my frustrations because he quickly sent Terrell away so we could have some quality time, plus he wanted to give me a stress reliever. That's just what the fuck he did and had my ass ready to sleep like a big ass baby. But before I could doze off, he crept in those three magical words. They were unexpected, but welcomed. Unsure if I was ready to say them back, I took a chance and let the positive response flow, then snuggled tightly under his arm. My favorite position to cuddle…

We may not have had the perfect love story, but I had definitely found my perfect guy…

The next morning I woke up to an unexpected text message. It was from Amon. My heart was beating a hundred miles per second and I was having trouble breathing.

"What the hell does he want?" I questioned silently as I opened the message.

Before I had a chance to read it, he was calling my cell. The only way I knew it was him was because it was coming from the same number that the text came from. I hesitated to answer it, but I figured if he really wanted to talk to me, he would have no problem coming to find me.

Creeping out of the bed, I tiptoed into the hallway to ensure a little privacy.

"Hello"

"Marina, I'm gonna keep this shit real brief," he explained. "If you can handle that issue out there or know somebody that can I would appreciate it."

"I, I, I really don't want to get involved," I stuttered.

"You have no fuckin' choice now! How the hell I don't know you ain't had nothin' to do with the money he stole from me in the first damn place?"

Amon's voice was getting louder which led me to believe that he wasn't playing.

"I didn't even know shit about it until I moved here," I lied.

"I really don't give a fuck when you found out! The only way to redeem ya self is to take care of this little situation."

"I can't do that shit myself," I complained.

"Stop with the bullshit Marina!" Amon warned. "I already know about ya boy getting shot, so I'm sure dude is thirstin' for a payback."

"Why can't you just do it?"

"Why the fuck you think? I can't risk getting locked up behind the shit! Everybody on the streets knows that that nigga got me! I don't need fools testin' my gangsta right now. I already got enough heat from murkin' his homeboy for his fuckin' dirt!"

Amon had an excellent point, but I was worried about him coming clean with the ends. I didn't want any of us to risk our freedom or lives for a personal vendetta that had nothing to do with us, and then not get paid.

"Look, if you agree to the shit, I'll have my boy bring you over fifty thousand to show you how serious I am."

"Why would you pay someone to do what you do so well by ya damn self?"

"I don't have time to answer all ya fuckin' questions, just say yeah or naw."

Knowing that Timothy would want in, I agreed. He told me that he would rush the money to me. When I attempted to give him my address, he cut me off and said not for me to worry about all that, then hung up on me.

When I came back into the room Timothy was still sleeping. It was five in the morning and the sun hadn't even come up yet.

As I looked at my man stretched across the bed, I wanted to dive back in to get me a little taste, but time didn't permit it. I had to get home to my children.

Shaking Timothy gently, I let him know that I was about to leave.

"Okay baby," he replied groggily. "I'll be home in a few. I just promised my moms that I would be here for breakfast. You sure you don't wanna stay?"

"I wish I could, but the kids will be up soon."

Timothy understood and kissed me goodbye. I left there with an awful lot of shit on my mind.

"Why didn't I just tell him that Amon called?" I quizzed myself all the way back to the house.

I could have called him and put him up to speed, but I decided to wait until he came home. At that point I didn't have much of a choice.

"Excuse me beautiful, your name must be Marina," a nice looking fella greeted as I approached my apartment.

"And who would like to know?" I probed checking my watch.

It was well after five in the morning which was a strange time to be out looking for me. He didn't seem to be a threat so I stood there and listened.

"Names aren't important," he flirted as he licked his lips and pressed them together. "At least not yet."

The unknown man came nearer and then slid me something.

"What is this?"

"Don't open that shit until you get in the house. When you do, you'll know exactly what's up. I'll contact you soon."

The handsome stranger disappeared before I could ask him another damn question.

"Now how the hell am I gonna explain this shit?" I thought to myself as I unlocked my door and relieved Cheryl of her babysitting duties.

"How is Timothy?"

"He's good."

"Was Terrell still there when you left?"

That question led me to believe that he hadn't come home. To avoid giving her a direct answer, I told her that I wasn't sure because I had been in Timothy's room all night.

"Was his car there when you left?"

"I'm sorry, I didn't even pay attention. It was dark and I got to my van as fast as I could. With all this crazy shit happening, my ass is paranoid."

Cheryl didn't press me any further. She seemed to be satisfied with my responses, so she dropped it and headed out.

Soon as she closed the door behind her, I ran to my room, bust the envelope open and spilled the contents out onto my bed.

"Oh my!" I screamed. "Oh my!"

Timothy

When Marina woke me to tell me that she was leaving I decided to get up. I slowly made my way to the bathroom to relieve my bladder before grabbing some breakfast. While I waited for my mama to let me know that my food was ready, I called my brother. We had some work to do and knowing him, when he left there the night before, he already had a head start. Listening to Terrell's phone ring four times, he finally answered.

"Yo wassup boe."

"Hey boe we need to have that conversation. Where you at?"

"I'm checking out a little sweet thang right now but I'll be round that way in a little bit. You gone be at mama's house or Marina's?"

"Just come by moms crib cuz I'll be here bout another hour before I go to Marina's."

"A'ight then, see you in a few."

In so many words Terrell just told me he had eyes on that bitch nigga. We weren't stupid. Anything we said on the phone could incriminate us so we learned to talk in code when we were just little kids. I wasn't trying to go to jail and neither was he.

I laid in my bed trying to formulate a plan when my mama called me down for breakfast. *Good!* I always thought better with a full stomach.

Moms threw down. She made eggs, bacon, sausage, country ham, grits, French toast and hot buttered biscuits. I was drooling at the mouth from the aroma of all the food mixed together. I made a hefty plate, blessed my grub and sat down to eat.

While I was stuffing my face, Terrell came in. He washed his hands, hooked himself up with a little of everything and took a seat at the table with us. It had been awhile since we all broke bread as a family. I loved it though. It had me looking forward to sharing many meals like that with Marina and the kids...

After we helped clean up, Terrell and I encouraged our mama to go to her room so she could catch up on her recorded shows. That gave us an opportunity to talk without her hearing our conversation. I made sure she was straight and didn't need anything before heading back to the kitchen.

"So what you find out?"

"Yo check it out. This nigga got a spot over in Fox Fire. He's staying with some other nigga and a female. I watched the house from the time I left here yesterday until you called me. I peeped the traffic coming and going through that house. It seems like they don't have shit jumpin' off over there between two and three in the morning. You know what that means right?'

"Dead hour nigga!"

"Yes indeed! I wanna sit and watch the house for another few days before we make a move though. I don't wanna go in there and get fucked up."

"That's a bet. Imma have Marina speak to her people up top to see if she can find out anything to help us out. This Amon cat seems to be the truth so maybe we can do this shit and chill out."

"Let me know what you find out boe. I'm game for whatever plan you come up with, but just know I wanna send that nigga to his maker."

"You got that boe. You have my word."

Talking to my brother made me feel better. He was always the more level headed one.

We had eyes on Colay's sorry ass now. I knew how Terrell got down. He was into all that incognito shit. He knew how to not be spotted wherever he went. You know that saying, "They'll be looking for ya ass in the daylight with a flashlight." Well you could look for that nigga all you wanted and you still wouldn't find him even if he was standing next to your ass. My brother was good with that shit.

I got myself together so I could get on over to Marina's house. I knew I dropped the "L" word on her the night before but I wasn't sure if she heard me. I really did love that woman. She was all a man could ask for and then some.

I tossed a bunch of clothes in my duffle bag and made my way downstairs. I saw Terrell getting ready to leave so I caught a ride with him over to my woman's house.

We pulled up just as Marina, I saw some pretty boy talking to her. She didn't see me so I was able to observe the scene.

The chat was brief so I didn't think shit of it, until I caught that nigga eye fucking my lady as she closed her door. I wondered who the fuck he was but I let it go because I wasn't back to one hundred percent just yet. Wasn't any need to start some beef that I couldn't finish right then and there. If he was important in any way then he would show up again and I would have no problems handling his ass if I needed to.

I stayed off in the cut and waited for dude to skedaddle before I used my key to go inside Marina's place. That's when I heard Marina yelling.

Knowing good and well I wasn't supposed to be straining myself, I took off running upstairs. Seeing that she wasn't in any immediate danger, I quickly eyed what was on the bed behind her. It had to be at least fifty stacks! I looked at her with a puzzled expression before I spoke.

"Yo you good? What's all this?"

"Babe have a seat and let me explain."

I did exactly what she asked me to do and listened intently as she told me about the call she got earlier from Amon. He basically told her that she had to handle the shit otherwise he would think she had something to do with her weak ass baby daddy stealing that money from him.

I started to get heated thinking about how he threatened my woman but I didn't say anything. She ended the story with telling me that Amon had sent some nigga over there with fifty stacks to show that he was serious about deading that nigga. So that explained the pretty boy nigga that I thought was hitting on my girl.

I let her finish before I brought her up to speed with what Terrell found out. We now had a starting point but I was soon about to finish this shit.

Marina

Right in the middle of counting the money, Cheryl called and asked to borrow my laptop to look up some information.

"Give me a second," I replied as I threw a blanket to cover the money. "I'll be right over."

Knowing that Cheryl would come over if I wasn't knocking at her door within five minutes, I hurried to fulfill her request.

"You know they had a shooting last night over on the south side," she acknowledged as she retrieved the computer from out of my grasp. "Someone was tryin' to rob my cousin's trap house."

Being wrapped up in Cheryl's drama, I found myself staying over there for a couple of hours. That's when my daughter called and asked where I was.

"I'm coming baby," I promised.

"I just have a few more things to look up," she informed me as she continued to peck away at the keys.

"Naw, you can use it. I'll come back later and get it."

Without looking up, Cheryl waved bye. I just laughed at her crazy ass and headed out the door.

"So, we meet again huh?"

It was the stranger that gave me the money. I almost didn't recognize him in his suit. He was looking real professional.

"If you're gonna keep sneakin' up on me like this, ya gonna at least tell me your name."

I felt myself flirting, but I couldn't help it. That man was making it difficult not to smile and bat my eyes.

Stepping so close to me that I could smell the Versace Eros cologne spewing from his clothes, I inhaled deeply and lost myself for a moment.

"Yeah, I was thinkin' the same thing ma'."

"Oh you were huh?"

"Yeah, that's why I came back so soon."

There he went with that licking of his damn lips. That motherfucker was seriously playing with me.

"Well?"

"My name is Devin, but everyone calls me DJ."

"Aight DJ, why are you all on me like that?"

"Because I'm invested in you."

"What the hell you mean by that?"

I pulled back a bit, but he was on me once again.

"Everywhere you go, I'll be there. I know all ya friends, where you work and even where ya lil' dude's momma stay," he revealed. "I see ya stayed ya fast ass over there all night. I meant to bust you up about that earlier."

"I'm glad you feel so comfortable tellin' me what the hell I can do or can't."

"My fault. I just see a beautiful young lady that takes care of her family. Now why would you leave them unattended with everything that's going on?"

"Oh, so ya questionin' my fuckin' parenting skills?" I replied defensively.

"No, not at all," he assured. "Just from now on, if you need to go somewhere, let me know so I can have someone watch ya house."

"So who's gonna watch me?"

"Oh, that would be my job."

Well damn, I didn't know I had security like that! Oh hell yeah. My day was getting better by the minute.

We went our separate ways, but not before he passed me his digits.

"In case of an emergency," he explained. "Or just if you need anything."

I couldn't make it back in the house good before Timothy got there and busted me with the money all over the bed. I had a good feeling he saw DJ outside too so I decided to explain everything the best I could without him overreacting.

Sitting him down, I danced around things we had already discussed then gradually got to the point. Soon as I mentioned DJ, his attitude shifted.

"Is that ole' boy I saw you out front with and then again just now?"

"Yeah, probably so."

"Damn, dude was all in ya grill like he was feelin' ya and shit."

The jealousy showed right through his expressions and I dared to tread that road. I let it ride and didn't reply to his insinuations.

"Even if he was, there's only one man I'm feelin'," I teased. "And he's right here."

As I dimmed the lights and got comfortable, Timothy locked the bedroom door.

"Ya tryna send me back to the hospital?"

"Naw, I just thought I could get me some real quick."

"We need to talk first Marina."

"What's up Tim?"

I scooted over on the bed and motioned him to join me.

Timothy gave me a peculiar look and began to grill me. He wanted to know what DJ had to do with the whole thing. I explained once again how he worked for Amon and he was getting paid to make sure we held up our end of the deal.

"How do you feel about takin' out the father of ya kids?"

That question was unexpected. I honestly hadn't thought of that.

"You really should have thought about that before accepting the money," he smirked with his head down. "If you wasn't so damn quick to be smiling up in dude's face, ya probably could've thought a lil' mo' clearly."

Sensing a tad bit of irritation, I moved closer to my man and rubbed his shoulders. Arguing was the last thing I wanted to do. We needed to be strong and united during our mission. He needed to stay focused. Hell, I did too because DJ was starting to distract me to the max. I knew if he kept popping up on me like he did, things were going to get uncomfortable between us. So, my best bet was to get Colay ten feet under and collect my ends as quickly as possible.

Timothy

I saw some hesitation when I asked Marina about killing her baby daddy. I hoped like hell that she wasn't gonna flake out on me. I didn't think she would though. Now that DJ cat, yeah I had to keep an eye on his ass. He was too close in Marina's face when I pulled up. I ain't like that shit. I would have no problems putting a bullet in his head except I didn't know who he was to Amon. If I knew I could kill him and get away with it, I would.

I stretched out on the bed lost in thought as Marina went to prepare the kids a snack. All of them were sitting quietly watching something on the Disney channel or so I thought. I heard a soft knock on the door before Mariela came in. I wondered what she wanted with me.

"Hey Tim. How are you feeling?"

"I'm ok Mariela. What's up?"

"You really like my mom don't you?"

"Yes I really do. Why do you ask me that?"

"I want you to marry my mom. You make her really happy and I like seeing my mom happy."

"Well I want to marry your mom too but we haven't talked about it yet. That's grown up stuff though."

"Ok but I'm going to tell my mom that I want her to marry you too. That's all I wanted to tell you though."

And with that she left. I wondered why Mariela came and told me that. I mean marrying Marina had crossed my mind but we'd only been dating a few months. It seemed like in the short time we'd been together we'd been through more stuff than most couples dealt with in a lifetime. I swear it didn't do nothing but make me want to protect her even more.

Her baby daddy was a certified nut job. What kinda nigga shoots another nigga over some pussy? If he would've treated her right then she never would've left his crazy ass.

Sitting there thinking about everything Marina told me about Colay only made me more ready to dead his ass. How could a man claim to love a person, marry and have babies with them then treat them like shit? I couldn't get past that shit, so once I got the chance to I was gonna make that nigga pay.

I went over the plan in my head about a hundred times making sure me and Terrell had all our bases covered. I needed to talk to this Amon dude. I needed to know if he had a crew that could come clean up behind us once the job was done. I made my way downstairs to talk to Marina.

The kids were still sitting in front of the TV when I heard the music playing in the kitchen. There was an old love song playing, SWV's Weak, and I heard Marina singing along. Damn she never ceased to amaze me. What couldn't this woman do? I listened to her sing until the song went off. I walked up behind her and wrapped my arms around her waist. I felt her shudder as I planted a kiss on the back of her neck. I knew that woman not only loved me, she was in love with me. I was in love with her as well.

"I love you baby."

"I love you too boo. Now what's up?"

"Damn is it that obvious that something is wrong?"

"Naw not necessarily wrong but I know you want something."

"You're right. I need to speak with Amon."

Marina whirled around to look at me like I was crazy. Before she could say anything I started to explain myself.

"Babe I only need to talk to him to see if he got a cleanup crew or something. Once we handle this business, we gone need to get rid of all the evidence."

"Damn good point. Ok I'll call him but let me explain why I need to get at him first. Amon isn't an easy dude to talk to especially when he don't know you."

I allowed Marina the space she needed to do what she had to do. I finished preparing the kids snacks as she left to go make that call. If that nigga had it like that, a cleanup crew shouldn't be hard to come by.

I heard Marina talking when she walked back into the kitchen and handed me the phone.

"Here. I got Amon on the line for you."

"Yo wassup boe? My name is-"

"Yeah I know who you are and all that so let's cut the small talk. Marina says you need a crew; I got that. When you doing this shit?"

"A few more days before the house needs to be cleaned up ya feel me? So when can that crew get here?"

"I already got em in the vicinity. Once the furniture is moved have Marina hit DJ's phone and the crew will come clean the house."

"Ok then good looking out boe."

Amon hung up and I was feeling good. He told me what I needed to hear and I was cool with that. I'm glad I didn't have to say all that extra shit on the phone. Amon was a smart man. Hell he must have been really clever to be making the type of money he was making and not get caught. I was satisfied with our conversation. Now it was time to go see what my baby was doing.

Marina had the smaller kids down for a nap and the older kids engrossed in a PlayStation game. Mariela, unlike the others, sat up reading a book.

While everyone was occupied, I took the opportunity to get me a little play from Marina. I looked over at her and she looked back at me. I winked at her and she knew what was up. I couldn't get enough of that woman. We snuck away for a quickie. All I needed was five minutes, ten at the most.

I came back downstairs feeling good and my woman was glowing. I could see myself living that life with her forever. When all the shit was over I was gonna make Marina my wife. There was no way in hell I was gonna let her get away from me. I was motivated to show her that all men weren't the same. I wasn't perfect, but I was one of a kind...

Marina

Having a strong feeling that Amon was going to go ham if I had Timothy call him, I dialed him first.

"I understand ya man is helpin' you and all but my contact is with you and you only," he explained slowly. "My digits are only for emergencies, that's why ya got DJ. Use that nigga. That's what he's there for."

Amon went on and hollered at Timothy but warned me that would be his one and only time. I understood his secrecy, especially because of the nature of the situation.

Soon after handling a little business, Timothy and I were up to some business of our own. He took care of me nicely and had me sporting a smile for the rest of the day.

Waiting for the children to pass out, I got showered and went in the bedroom expecting to pick up where we had left off.

"Where are you going?" I questioned Timothy once I saw he was fully clothed and slipping on his shoes.

"I gotta meet Terrell over at the spot to talk to a few folks," he explained. "I need to make sure everything is in order before we do this shit ma."

Feeling disappointed, I told him I understood and sucked the shit up. He kissed me and told me that he would be back before I knew it.

Calling Cheryl over, I felt like having a drink or two.

"I'll be over there in just a second," she assured. "I need to fill you in on ya man's brother! Ugh! I'm so tired of his lies! I just know he fuckin' with that Tina bitch on the front side of the complex!"

"Don't trip Cheryl," I smirked. "You know if that nigga cheatin' that shit is gonna come out sooner or later, especially if the shit is goin' on up in our apartments."

My homegirl came right over and went on to tell me about all Terrell's late nights and phone calls at odd hours. When I told her it was most likely about some shit him and Timothy were into, she revealed it had been going on way before the shooting.

"I know something that will make you feel better."

"What Marina?"

"Tim is about to run some errands, so I was thinking that a little shopping would do us both some good."

"Who the fuck got money for all that?"

"Don't worry about all that," I clowned. "Just have ya ass ready by noon tomorrow."

Even though I had only known Cheryl a short time, we had become very close. She had always been there when I needed her for anything, especially when I needed help with the kids. I thought it was only right to help her out. The hard times had been upon her and I was finally in the position that I could do something nice in return. I had the perfect gift in mind.

To get a better idea of what else she needed in her home, I walked her across the path.

"You really need to take ya ass in the house Marina," Cheryl laughed. "You can't even walk straight."

Feeling woozy, I stepped back a bit and began to lose my balance. All of a sudden I was in a pair of strong arms. I knew who it was right away due to his cologne.

"You gotta be a bit more careful Marina," DJ warned with a crooked grin.

"Who's ya friend Marina?" Cheryl quickly questioned.

"Oh, this is my friend DJ," I introduced.

Cheryl's eyes seemed as if they were going to buck out of their sockets. She stood there quietly as DJ whispered a few words in my ear before walking away.

"You need to be careful every time ya step ya ass out that front door. Now, I'm here to make sure the job gets done, but I can't be out here babysittin' you. Even if you are the most beautiful woman I have ever laid eyes on."

His comment had me in a daze. He was so slick with his words that they had me tripping.

"Naw, naw, naw Marina," Cheryl clowned. "That motherfucker right there is feeling ya ass and I do mean literally! Did you see the way dude was lookin' at you?"

I tried to explain who he was, but she wasn't trying to hear shit that fell from my mouth. She began to tease me so I had to check her ass.

"Look, the shit is funny now, but don't mention that shit in front of Tim!"

"I wouldn't dare!"

We stood outside talking a bit before Timothy walked up on us.

"Did I miss something?"

"Yes you did," I teased with a kiss to his lips. "Now come on inside this house so you can get reacquainted with my vertical slit."

"Y'all so damn nasty!" Cheryl pouted as she went into her empty apartment.

"Naw, not yet," Timothy laughed as we opened up our door to enter. "But when we get up in here it's on and poppin'."

Wasting no time, my man took me to the bedroom and took care of my every need. He had me screaming so loud he had to put the pillow over my head to calm me down.

"Oh, ya real funny Tim," I giggled. "I couldn't breathe."

"So, I know the kids heard that shit Marina!"

"I'll just tell them that it was the TV."

Timothy just shook his head at me and continued to laugh.

"That's just why I love you girl," he admitted.

"Why's that?"

"Because you always keep me smiling."

Quickly grabbing my hand, he escorted me to the bathroom.

"Ready for round two?"

"Oh yes, yes I am."

We climbed into the shower and did it in there and then we took it to the bed. We created yet another memory that was worthy of praise. It was incredible and I savored our physical union until the moment I passed out...

Timothy

Marina wanted me to break her off with a quickie before I left. As bad as I wanted to, I had to wait until I came back. I just knew she was gonna go ham on me when I told her I had to meet up with Terrell but she shocked me and didn't say shit. I promised her that when I got back I would take care of her real proper so she was cool.

I called Terrell to have him come pick me up and he told me to come meet him around the front of the complex. I didn't know why he was at Tina's spot. Cheryl would kill his ass if she knew he was there. I was hoping that he was using her for something and he wasn't smashing the chick. Cheryl had already caught Terrell with his dick in Tina's mouth, literally. Cheryl beat the shit out of that girl and then turned around and went after my brother.

Tina made it clear that from that point on, whenever she was around Terrell she was gonna try her best to get with him any way she could. I know my brother wasn't over there trying to bust a nut when he had a good woman at home. I couldn't help but shake my head at my brother's antics. He was really on some other shit right now.

I knocked on Tina's door and I heard her loud ass yelling that it was open. When I walked in I was shocked! It looked like a mini command center or some shit. Ok I'm bullshitting but it did have a lot of computers everywhere. Maybe Terrell wasn't on no bullshit after all. Turns out ole 'Good Time' Tina was really smart and good with computers. She could get any information you wanted on anybody. *Well who would have known that shit?*

Terrell explained to me that it was how he always stayed a few steps ahead of everybody. He didn't mean to get caught fucking around with Tina that time but he had heard rumors that she was better than Superhead herself so he wanted to try her out. He didn't expect Cheryl to come around the corner and catch them in the act. After that he stayed as far away from Tina while in Cheryl's presence.

Tina was click clacking away at the computers key looking a real certified nerd when she hollered out BINGO! We both ran over to her to see what she was so happy about.

"Yo wassup? What you find out?"

"I know that there's three people in the house; A Miss Tenaiya Smith, Christopher Smith and Colay Smith. Christopher Smith is the first cousin to Colay Smith and Tenaiya is Christopher's wife. They have two young children.

According to what I found out though, this is not their primary residence. I was able to find several police reports and court records for Christopher Smith. It stated that he was considered a drug dealer, moved major weight and just got finished doing a seven year bid at Central Prison in Raleigh.

No wonder Colay brought his ass down here. With all the money that he stole from Amon he could easily help his cousin get back in the game.

"Well looky here. These motherfuckers are more stupid than I thought. No wonder his dumb ass got caught."

"What? What you find?"

"This nigga been communicating via text message to some cat back in Chicago about a shipment. Even though he tried to use some sort of code, it wasn't discreet enough. Hell even my simple ass could figure this shit out."

"Who's the cat from Chicago he dealing with?"

I watched Tina tap on the keys a few more times before she came up with a name.

"Seems like he's dealing with some cat named Amon. No last name."

Terrell and I looked at each other. This shit was starting to get weird. I wondered if this Christopher dude knew about the bounty on his cousin's head and was trying to collect it himself. My mind started to wander over different possibilities of the connection. Terrell must have been thinking the same shit as me because at the same time we both said: Marina.

After getting that tad bit of information from Tina, Terrell and I made our way back to Marina's spot. I needed her to call Amon again. We had to see what he wanted us to do about this Christopher cat. I didn't want to get caught up in no extra shit. My plan had to be foolproof. We had thought of every single scenario possible and had a plan of action for each one. There was no room for fuck ups.

Marina was just making the kids dinner when we got there. She saw the look in our eyes when we came in so she knew it was something serious. I waited for her to finish setting the kids up with their food before we headed up to her room.

"Why y'all looking like something is wrong?"

"Yo ma shit just got real!"

Me and Terrell ran down what we found out, leaving out the fact that Tina was the one who got us the information. After relaying all the information to Marina, she sighed deeply.

"Man this is some heavy shit. What if his cousin knows about the bounty? And kids? I don't know if I'm cool with y'all hurting little kids."

We had no intentions on hurting any kids but knowing what we knew then, shit just got way more complicated. We gave Marina some privacy to call Amon while we figured out our next move.

Marina

After all the shit Timothy and his brother told me, I didn't know what to think. We had to come up with something totally different.

"Why don't you call Amon and see what you can find out about Christopher?" Terrell inquired.

"Because that fool is private and the last time I spoke to him he made that shit crystal clear!"

Timothy came and comforted me when he saw that I was a little shaken up about the new information. I had six precious children to think about and that Christopher Smith character seemed to be a nigga that terrorized the streets. Sure I had a gun and I knew how to use it, but I never had to. Thing was, I had a good feeling I was about to.

"Let me call DJ and ask his opinion on all of this," I informed them as I dialed his number.

"What's up Marina?"

"I wanted to talk to you."

"Well where did you wanna do that at because I see you got company right now?"

That motherfucker didn't miss a damn beat. His ass was on me so tight I was starting to get irritated but I stayed focused.

"Why don't you tell me since you seem to have all the answers," I clowned. "I need to talk to Amon too."

Timothy gave me a dirty look as if he didn't like how the conversation was going. I rolled my eyes and held my hand out to tell him to chill.

"I'll be outside in ten minutes."

When I hung up, Timothy and Terrell began to question me. They wanted to know what the deal was with DJ. I explained to them once again what I knew about him.

"Well I don't trust dude," Terrell acknowledged as he stood to his feet.

Timothy was right behind him as if they were going with me outside to meet with DJ.

"Where y'all going?" I smirked. "He aint gonna talk to me with y'all there. So either stay in the house or go over to Cheryl's."

As soon as my man twisted his lips up to say something slick, I cut his ass off.

"Either we gonna do this or not," I spoke in a serious tone. "It's not gonna work if we don't cooperate with Amon and DJ. That's the only way we're gonna get paid. Now, we can dead this nigga and be done with it or we can do as they ask and get rewarded for getting rid of the piece of shit."

Terrell wanted to just kill him and not deal with the Chicago kingpins but Timothy convinced him to be patient. Although he had not seen me in street mode, my man knew I could hold my own.

"Take ya heat Marina," Timothy demanded. "I would feel a whole lot better if I knew you had it."

"Oh, I am. I don't know these niggas from Adam, so I'm on my shit."

After grabbing my handbag, I stuffed it with all the necessary items to defend myself as well as my cell.

"If you guys leave these apartments, text me and let me know!" Timothy stated before kissing me in the mouth. "I'm gonna stay here with the kids and hold shit down."

"Gotcha," I replied with another lip smack.

Heading outside, I thought about going to the bathroom but my cell ringing threw me off.

"Hey DJ, I'm outside. Where are you?"

"I'm in the parking lot on the north side. I'm in an all-black Denali. I have my lights on and my shit is running so come on."

"Where are we going?"

"Didn't you say you wanted to talk to Amon?"

"Ain't he in Chicago?"

DJ began to laugh as I approached the truck. He was standing outside of the passenger door waiting to help me in.

"Before I get in, I need to know where the hell you're takin' me!"

"Are you coming or not?"

DJ smiled and assured me that I was in safe hands. I didn't feel endangered at all, so I decided to hop in.

"So, I take it you don't want to go to Chicago," DJ teased. "Let me see if I can get him to do a video chat. If not, we may have to go to him."

My palms began to sweat as he got Amon on the line. The conversation was short and I knew by the way he eyed me that he didn't agree to Skype.

"I may as well take you back to ya crib, unless you want to hit ya dude up and tell him what's up."

Damn, I was feeling torn. I didn't want to contact Timothy and he didn't go for it. There was no way he would. But there was no way I could travel twelve hours and not let him know where I was. He had my kids. I had to call.

"Fuck that! I'm gonna text him," I decided out loud as I sent the message.

We went and gassed up while I waited for Timothy to respond. It didn't take long...

After we got some petro, DJ informed me that we were going to the airport to get there quicker. I was glad but I really wasn't prepared for a commercial flight.

"This ain't Fayetteville Regional," I smirked as we pulled up to a private airstrip. "Where are we?"

"Eastover Air Ranch Airport," DJ replied.

Asking no more questions, I followed him to the small fancy jet waiting for us on the runway. We climbed the stairs and boarded the extravagant plane.

"Good Evening," the female attendant greeted as we took our seats. "Would you like something to eat or a drink?"

"Yeah, I didn't get a chance to grub," DJ responded with a rub to his stomach. "What ya got tonight?"

"We have chicken or fish."

"I'll take the chicken and some Courvoisier," he answered then looked at me. "Would you like anything?"

"I guess I'll have the same."

I tried my best to suppress the excitement filling my body. The plane was like no other I had been on. I felt like I was royalty. I hurried to get comfortable and stay calm.

While waiting for the food, DJ started questioning me about my relationship with Timothy. It began with general questions but by the time we finished our meal and had our second drink, the interrogation became personal.

"So what do you look for in a man Marina?"

"Nothing in particular. As long as they're respectful, loyal and love me and my kids, I'm cool."

"So no requirements in the bedroom area?"

Damn! That shit threw me and had my ass stuttering. I tried my best not to look at his luscious lips or defined physique while answering him. The alcohol was definitely affecting me.

"Not really," I laughed. "As long as we're both satisfying one another then I have no complaints."

Scooting closer to me, DJ began to compliment me on my hair. Taking his finger, he took one of my curly locks and twisted it around his finger.

"Damn, if you were my girl..."

"If I were your girl what?"

"Did I just say that shit out loud?" I quizzed myself quietly.

It was too late and there was no taking that last statement back. My palms began to perspire and I tried to create a larger space in between us.

"Why ya runnin'?"

"I'm not."

"Am I making you nervous?"

"A little," I admitted shyly.

"Why is that?"

"Because you're a little intimidating."

"I know you're not scared of me, so what cha' sayin'?"

"You seem to be a force to be reckoned with on the streets."

"Well, we ain't on the streets."

"You right."

Now I was stuck not knowing what to say. DJ was so far in my face I thought he was going to try me.

"Buckle up, we're about to touch the pavement in less than five," the flight attendant said over the intercom.

Feeling the plane descend, I clicked my belt and sat up straight.

"Damn that was fucked up timing," DJ complained as he followed suit.

We didn't get off the plane, instead the door opened and Amon stepped on. I so wasn't expecting that.

"Hey Marina," he greeted with a hug. "Ya lookin' good girl."

"Thanks Amon."

When we pulled back off, he explained the do's and don'ts about contacting him. He was a very private person and I understood that.

We talked about how handy I was with a gun. I didn't understand where the conversation was going until Amon told me what would happen if Timothy was caught. It was cold hearted how he put it, but it most certainly gave me a reality check.

Amon let me know that he could wind up in jail or worse, dead. I knew the consequences but had little choice in the matter. Colay had been coming hard so I had to do something to protect my family and that included Timothy.

"If you did it yourself, it could be easily ruled as self-defense," Amon clarified. "You have a restraining order against him and there are plenty of records of abuse. Am I correct?"

The fewer people involved the less of a risk it was. I got that. But, to envision myself laying the father of my kids to rest was a humdinger.

"Just think about it Marina. I don't want to pressure you in anyway. If you still want ya dude to handle it, that's cool too. I just thought I'd give you some options that would possibly keep your family together. Let us just go back to North Carolina so I can talk with Tim face to face."

Timothy

"ARE YOU FUCKING KIDDING ME? You gotta go to Chicago to talk to this cat?" I yelled into the phone knowing that my girl couldn't hear me.

I got that bullshit ass text from Marina about leaving. Right then I was not feeling my woman being gone with some nigga I didn't know shit about. I didn't understand why Amon couldn't just answer a simple ass question. Although I didn't agree with it, I let my baby go handle her business. I made sure to tell her to keep in contact with me at all times so I knew what was going on.

In the meantime, I had an agenda of my own. If Tina could find out that Amon was connected to Christopher then she could tell me some shit about Amon and maybe even this DJ cat. If I found out some bullshit along the way then I would handle it as I saw fit. I tended to the kids and got them situated before I let my thoughts consume me.

A few hours later I got a text from Marina. She let me know they made it to Chicago safely and she was on her way to see Amon. Wondering how she got there so fast, I asked her. She said they flew up there on a private charter plane.

Well that nigga had more surprises then a little bit didn't he?

First he sent some strange nigga to follow and watch Marina then he had private planes flying her out of the state? Shit was getting crazy.

I couldn't sleep after I got that text from Marina. I was anxious as to what was going on in that meeting and if she was ok or not. I couldn't let my emotions get the best of me right then, so I rolled a blunt to mellow out. While I was smoking Terrell knocked on the door. I gave him a quick rundown of what was going on with Marina.

"So she had to go all the way to Chicago boe?"

"Yeah man and I ain't feeling this shit but I gotta let my baby handle her business."

"So when is she supposed to be back?"

"I ain't gotta clue but if something happens to her….."

I couldn't even finish my sentence, so I just left it how it was. Now more than anything I wanted Colay's ass dead. He fucked with the right one when he shot me.

My brother and I jumped on my PlayStation 3 to pass the time. I couldn't keep wondering about what Marina was doing. I just had to trust that she was handling her business. Terrell stayed for about four hours. It was just when he was about to leave that I heard the locks clicking.

Both of us pulled our heat out until we realized it was Marina. We relaxed until we noticed she was followed by two men. She didn't look scared or in danger so I lowered my gun as did my brother but I kept my finger on the trigger. Marina walked over to me and took the gun from my hand. She stood on her tip toes to kiss me and I relaxed completely.

"Hey babe we all needed to talk. I knew Amon needed to talk to you as well you to him but I knew I needed to break the ice. I went to Chicago, talked to him and convinced him to come with me back here. This meeting is for everyone to lay their cards out on the table."

"Are you sure?"

"Yeah babe, I'm sure. I'll leave you men to your business and I'll be upstairs minding my own."

With that she made the introductions, kissed me and went straight upstairs. I eyeballed Amon and DJ. So did Terrell. I knew my brother was on the same page as me so I wasn't worried. It was those two shady niggas that I was worried about. It was time to get down to business.

"So Amon I'm not sure if Marina let you know or not but what are we supposed to do about this Christopher cat?"

"Ahhhh. A man who gets straight to it. I like that. Christopher is not your concern though. He is now my problem but I know that you and I have a common dislike for Colay."

"That we do. What do you suggest we do?"

"Go forward with your plan. You won't have to worry about Christopher or his wife once you decide to execute it so long as DJ is contacted at least 24 hours prior."

"And the clean up?"

"That too will be taken care of. If all goes well, you'll be paid your money and I will be out of your way. The only reason I'm extending this offer to you is because Marina is an old and dear friend to me. Had she not been, I would've wasted no time handling her either."

"Is that a threat?"

"No threats. Just telling the truth. Look at it from my point of view. A man and woman you've known for almost all your life suddenly change. Marina leaves Colay as well as leaves town and then Colay disappears. I find out that I have a lot of money missing and the only two who can tell me about it are nowhere to be found. Now I hate to go searching for shit that belongs to me so when Marina called I took the opportunity presented to me. If Marina was as loyal as I knew her to be, giving up Colay wouldn't be shit for her. She has been proven worthy. You have a very rare woman there. Treat her right."

We talked a bit more and I came to see that Amon wasn't a bad dude. He was just very guarded and he had every right to be. If I was running something huge in a city like Chicago then I would be too. Now that I knew everything was all good, I let our guests go about their business, locked up the house and climbed the stairs to where my woman lay at. When I got to the bedroom door I saw Marina already fast asleep. I still couldn't believe that amazing woman was mine.

I quickly took my clothes off leaving only my boxers on and climbed into the bed. I guess when my weight shifted the mattress it caused Marina to wake up because she looked at me with a smile before she dozed back off.

I positioned my body behind hers and pulled her close to me. That was my life now. It couldn't have been more complete.

Marina

Feeling a bit overwhelmed, I closed my eyes and relaxed until we made it back to North Carolina. That's when it was time to make some serious decisions but I needed my other half for that.

We hopped back in DJ's ride and made our way back to the apartments. When we stepped in, the expression on Timothy's face was priceless. I quickly introduced them and kept it pushing up to my bedroom.

I must have passed out while waiting on my man. I couldn't wait to find out how the meeting went. That's why when morning arrived I was all in his face with a million and one questions...

"So, what happened?"

"Everything is under control Marina."

Timothy wasn't going into detail, so I pushed the issue. That shit didn't do anything but make him jump up out the bed and get dressed.

"Damn, where ya goin' at this hour?"

"I got shit to take care of so we can handle this business. The sooner I do, the sooner we can go on with our lives in peace."

Timothy kissed me on the cheek and headed to the door.

"So that's it? I don't get a little taste or nothing?" I pouted as I gave him a sneak peek of my goodies.

"Oh now ya wanna play dirty huh?" Timothy laughed as he came right back out his shirt and pants. "How can I say no to that shit right there?"

Climbing on top of me, he reminded me how much he loved me and that he would do anything for me and my kids. While the sincerity in his eyes convinced my heart, his hardness below persuaded his way into my stash.

Timothy took me on a trip without leaving the house and I was grateful but exhausted. I couldn't move. I heard the shower run. Then minutes later I felt a kiss on my forehead.

"Get up baby, I'm hungry!" he whispered as he persisted to push my body back and forth until I opened my eyes.

I knew how he got when he wanted something to eat, so I went ahead and climbed out of the bed.

"If you think I'm going in the kitchen and making you something at this time of the morning you're sadly mistaken mister," I yawned. "The sun aint even up yet!"

"Naw, I wouldn't do that to you after you took care of me like you did baby. Your performance received ten stars," he teased.

"Okay, thank you baby," I replied kissing him on the cheek and climbing back into the bed.

"So I guess you're not riding with me to Mickey D's huh?" he questioned one last time before jingling my keys to the van. "Aight, I'm out baby."

I swear Timothy wasn't out the door two minutes before my cell started ringing. His ass couldn't go ten feet away without calling.

"What did you forget baby?" I blurted out as soon as I connected the call.

"I forgot to kiss you goodnight," DJ whispered into the phone.

"Stop playin'! And stop fuckin' spyin' on me!" I spat and I pressed the 'end' button. DJ called right back.

"What is it? You called me for something. Get to the fuckin' point would ya?" I snapped.

"Come outside. Amon forgot to give you something," he revealed. "It's something you'll need in case of an emergency."

Realizing that there was no way around it, I slid on my shorts and house shoes before I stepped out into the darkness. I didn't have time to put on a bra, so I folded my arms across my chest.

"Why didn't you put on a jacket baby?" DJ asked as he came to me. "You gon' freeze to death out here."

"Well I only planned on staying out here a second. You said you just had to give me something. What is it?" I hurried him.

"Damn, can I at least get a hug first?"

"If I give you one will you promise to leave me be?"

"Yes, I promise I won't bother you unless it's urgent!" he swore and crossed his heart.

Pulling me into him, my erect nipples brushed up against his stomach. But that was not the only thing standing up.

"Damn DJ!" I smirked as I snatched away. "For real?"

After repositioning his stiff one, DJ apologized and told me that he couldn't help himself. My thoughts were all over the place and I nearly forgot to ask him about what Amon forgot to give me.

"Okay DJ, where is it?"

Digging in his pocket, he drew out a small piece of folded yellow paper. He told me that it was a list of numbers to call just in case something went wrong. He told me never to use my name, only a location.

DJ seemed to be rambling on and it was cold outside. Not only that, but Timothy would be coming back at any minute. I was sure DJ knew that shit too. He just wanted to start some shit between me and my man, but I had news for his ass. It wasn't going to happen.

I quickly bid his ass a farewell and hurried myself back into the house. Just as I was about to climb back in bed, I smelled a faint whiff of DJ's cologne. I knew for sure if I did then Timothy would too.

Stripping down to nothing, I ran my ass through the shower within two minutes. When I got my pajamas on Timothy was coming in the room with food. I wasted no time to eat. I was tired and no good after that.

The rest of the morning was history. I didn't get out of bed until the afternoon...

Timothy

After my shower, I found Marina knocked out. I hurried to get ready and was out the door in less than 20 minutes. It was time to make some moves. First thing was first. I had to check in with Terrell. He was supposed to be peeping out the spot where Colay was posted up at. We were gonna make our move in two days.

Even though I wasn't fully healed, I couldn't wait any longer now that I had met with Amon. Personally I wanted to do the shit so everything could go back to normal.

That DJ cat was starting to get under my skin too. I saw the way he looked at Marina when he was around. Even though I saw the shit only a few times, it was already a few times too many for me. The faster we got the job done, the faster that nigga would be gone. All I had to do was finalize the plans I had with Terrell and shit would be gravy. I hit Terrell up and told him to meet me out front.

"Yo bro wassup? I thought after last night you'd be hemmed up in the house with Marina."

"Nigga whatever. Let's get down to business."

We cracked a few more jokes on the way to Fox Fire. I wanted Terrell to show me the house during the day so I could be sure to have all angles covered when we came back. We had it set that we would hit the house between two and four in the morning. Those hours were considered to be when a person was sleeping the hardest. I was banking on the fact that Colay's bitch ass would be having forty winks right about then so it would be easy to do.

We made a left turn into Fox Fire and kept going straight. The house was just two blocks up on the left hand side. We pulled over half a block up so we wouldn't be spotted. Terrell and I made small talk as we watched some of the traffic going in and out of Colay's house for a few hours when a familiar car pulled up.

What the fuck?

It was Marina's car. Instead of jumping to conclusions I waited to see what was going on.

I watched the door to the house open just as Marina was getting out of her van. I spotted Colay coming out the door towards Marina. I wondered what the fuck was going on until I saw her open up the back door to her van. The kids were in the back and it seemed as though they wanted to see their father. I was pissed that Marina didn't even bother to tell me that she knew where this nigga stayed at or the fact that she brought the kids over there. I was mad but at the same time I couldn't be mad, if that made any sense. I mean, he was their father.

I sat and watched, patiently waiting to see if anything would happen when I got a text from Marina.

Babe: Hey I'm at Colay's....don't be mad but I have a reason as to why I'm here

Me: Yeah what's that?

Babe: We needed to know what was going on in the house right?

Me: Yeah so?

Babe: What better way than for me to bring my kids over so I could check it out.

Me: Yeah a'ight.

At first I was pissed when she said that shit, but then I thought about it. My woman was a fucking genius. I didn't even think about dude wanting to see his kids as a way into the house. I hoped that Marina would be able to give me a full layout of everything when she left there. I had Terrell crank the car up so we could ride out. I knew when my woman came home later she'd have something good for me. Well I'd have something good for her too. I knew Terrell was dying to say something to me so I asked him.

"What boe? Why you keep looking at me out the side of ya eye and shit?"

"Do you think it was a good idea to leave Marina alone there with the kids?"

"That nigga may be stupid but I don't think he'd do anything to his kids."

"Never say never boe. That's all I'm saying."

I let what my brother said sit on my mind. Would Colay be that cold blooded and hurt his kids? I had to think that as a father he wouldn't do that shit but now since Terrell put that shit in my mind, I couldn't get it out. I shot Marina a text as we were pulling up to the house when I saw Tina. She was yelling out Terrell's name trying to get his attention. At the same time Cheryl was stepping out her door.

She heard Tina calling my brother's name and made a beeline towards her. Terrell didn't even throw the car in park before he jumped out. Luckily I was able to put it in neutral and climb over into the driver's seat to park it. I jumped out and ran towards the ladies because it was sure to be a showdown between them. I could hear everybody yelling at each other but couldn't make out what they were saying.

I watched as Terrell was trying his best to keep both women apart. I jogged over and grabbed Cheryl by the arm.

"Come on Cheryl. You don't need to be fighting out here."

"Naw fuck that shit! After I whoop that bitch's ass imma whoop ya brother's ass! I've had enough of his shit."

"It ain't what you think and before you say I'm defending my brother, it ain't even about that. This is business Cheryl."

"Business? What the fuck kind of business involves this hoe running up on my man every chance she gets?"

"You don't need to know all that shit right now. All you need to know is that he ain't fucking that girl and you bringing some unwanted attention our way right now."

She snatched her arm away from me and stomped off. I didn't need that shit right then. If people started calling the police and they started sniffing around there I might have had to put my plans on hold. There was no way I was gonna do that, so I had to smooth shit out.

After Cheryl took her ass on, I went over to where my brother and Tina stood.

"Man boe what the fuck is going on? Why you out here hollering out niggas names and shit? You know his girl don't like you Tina. You tryna start some shit."

"Look boe fuck that broad. I ain't tryna start shit but I do have something that both of y'all need to see."

She shoved the paper she had in my face. I scanned over it with Terrell reading it over my shoulder. At the same time we both hollered out what the fuck! It seemed as though that DJ cat who was supposed to be working for Amon was also working with Colay.

Ain't this some ol' complicated shit?

So now not only did I have to worry about one shady ass nigga, but two. That was some bullshit.

I wondered how I was gonna bring the shit up to Marina. That news just made things worse. I had to worry about whether or not we'd even be able to pull the shit off without worrying about DJ's fake ass. I knew there was something about him that I didn't like.

Shit! I had a ton of things weighing heavy on my mind but I pushed them to the side for the time being. I was about to go in the house and make dinner for my family.

The conversation Marina and I needed to have that night was going to be heavy. It would also solidify our union. I trusted my woman to the fullest and after that night, she was gonna be my wife.

Marina

When I finally dragged myself out of bed, Timothy was gone. My kids were acting like they were starving and just had to have me fix them something, so I went ahead and hooked them up.

"Mom, when can we go see daddy?" Latrell, my oldest son asked as I made lunch.

I stayed silent and continued to cut the sandwiches and place them on the plates. Trying not to snap on him, I glanced at him and smiled. I had a bright ass idea.

"You wanna call him?"

"Can I?"

"Yeah, you sure can," I laughed. "But I don't want him comin' over here, so get his address and tell him that I will bring you over there after you guys finish eating."

"Cool."

After grabbing my cell, a pen and a piece of paper, I dialed Colay's number and handed my son the phone. I swear they weren't on the line ten seconds before I heard him yelling.

"Mom, daddy wants to talk to you!"

"Damn, that's just what I didn't want to do," I mumbled.

I came from the kitchen and ran right into my son who was holding my cell out laughing. I didn't see shit funny. After I snatched the phone out of his hand he got the picture and skedaddled his ass out of the room.

"Hey Colay," I choked from the bad taste his name left in my mouth.

"Hey Marina. I hear the kids wanna see they daddy huh? That nigga ain't provided that stable foundation he claimed to huh?"

"I didn't let our son call you to listen to all that. So do you want to see them or not?"

"I'm on my way!"

"Oh hell to the naw! We done been there and done that shit! My complex already done trespassed you off the property."

"Well bring them over here," Colay suggested.

I had him to text me the address and I was over there with the kids within the next half hour. Once I made it, I thought about Timothy. I hadn't told him shit. There I was, again making decisions like I wasn't part of a team. I couldn't help it. All that shit was new to me. When I was married to Colay, I was definitely flying solo.

Luck was on my side. Timothy didn't trip about it. In fact he was cool with it once I told him that I had the full inside scoop to give him when I got home.

I made the visit as quick as possible. While Colay was busy entertaining the kids, I gathered as much information as I could. He was so damn geeked that I brought them that he paid me no mind. That made it easy as pie to scope every room in the house.

Once I was satisfied, I rushed the kids to the van. We had only been there about forty-five minutes so the younger ones had an attitude. Now the older ones, they beat me outside. They saw right through their dad's bullshit.

When we got back to the house, Timothy had dinner made. We fed everyone and I went to bathe the kids while my man took care of the kitchen.

While coming down the stairs, I heard Terrell's voice. I knew they were waiting on me to come and join them so that I could fill them in on what I found out at Colay's.

"So they got that shit set up like Fort Knox or naw?"

"Or naw! That shit is so laid back. All them niggas they got up in there look lazy as fuck. They either eating, smoking weed or on the damn video games."

"Do they have cameras?" Timothy questioned.

"I did notice a security system, but that shit looked outdated like a motherfucker!"

"Well, we can't take any fuckin' chances," Terrell warned as he paced the floor. "I'm ready to dead this nigga!"

The interrogation began and I answered the brothers as best as I possibly could. They needed to know how many bedrooms, exits and people were occupying the crib. Now when they quizzed me about DJ, I began stuttering.

"What does he have to do with this?"

"That's what I'm trying to find out." Timothy stated with a twinge of jealousy.

"Imma leave up out of here on that note boe," Terrell laughed giving his brother a fist pound. "After you guys finish with ya chat, get at me so we can handle this shit as quick as possible. On the real tho'."

Timothy waited for Terrell to shut the door behind him before he came to me with his feelings on DJ. I couldn't say much because there wasn't shit between us. Not wanting his insecurities to interfere with our plan or relationship, I put all that shit to rest.

"I really don't give a damn if dude is feelin' me Tim. My heart belongs to you and you along with the space my kids are already occupying, there ain't room for nobody else babe."

"That's all I needed to hear baby."

Escorting me to the bedroom, Timothy squeezed my hand and gave me a quick wink. That let me know what time it was. Well at least I thought I did. He proved me so fucking wrong when he got up out of the bed after the first round. Hell, I was just getting started.

"Where you goin'?"

"You know I gotta go meet Terrell," he explained as he went to wash his ass.

"Ain't it a little late for all that?"

"That's when the best business is conducted baby," Timothy yelled out from the shower. "Don't trip. If something goes down tonight, I'll let you know."

My chest began to pound with anxiety. Just the thought of Colay actually being dead had me nervous but I knew it had to be done. I was too far in to even think about backing out. Amon made that perfectly clear during our last conversation.

Tension was getting the best of me when Timothy eased up beside me with his wet body that smelled oh so good. I tried to turn around and embrace him, but he slid from my grip and teased me.

"Oh no no baby," he smiled. "We'll have plenty of time for that later on. That is if ya ass ain't knocked the hell out."

"If I am, wake me the fuck up!"

I giggled and blew him a kiss as he got dressed.

"Don't worry, I will."

Feeling bored after my man left, I decided to call Cheryl to see if she was still up. She answered on the first ring yelling about the fight that she got into with Tina.

"Tim ain't tell you?" Cheryl questioned with an attitude.

"Naw, girl."

"Wasn't him and his brother just over there a while ago?"

"Yeah, but I was in the room with the kids," I explained not wanting to go into details.

Cheryl was upset and coming at me like I was hiding something. Which I was, but not what she was thinking. I couldn't think of a damn thing to say to calm her down, so I told her I was coming over with a bottle. That shut her ass up...

"We gotta stop meeting like this," DJ chuckled as he approached me before I could knock on Cheryl's door. "Oh, ya got some Hennessy too? You know you don't need to drink to get drunk right? Right now you need to stay on point for whatever."

"For whatever huh?" I giggled.

"Yeah, for whatever," DJ repeated as he gently placed an unexpected kiss on my lips.

Stepping back from him, I hit him with a fucked up expression.

"Damn, did I overstep my boundaries?"

"Yes, you did."

"I'm sorry Marina, I thought you were ready."

Without waiting for a response, he turned around and walked away. I didn't know what to make out of it.

Unaware of DJ's angle, I erased the questions dancing in my dome and went inside Cheryl's to get my mind right...

Timothy

It was almost D-Day. We had exactly twenty-four hours left before Colay's ass was gone for good. I had plans to take care of DJ afterwards at no extra charge to Amon. If I had a snake ass nigga in my camp and another nigga took care of him, I'd be grateful.

Terrell and I left the crib about one in the morning to head to Colay's. That was the last time we'd be there before everything went down.

We rode quietly to Fox Fire, both of us lost in our own thoughts. I don't know what my brother was thinking but I know for damn sure what I was thinking. After we put all this shit behind us, I was gonna put a ring on it. Yep! Ya boy would officially be off the market. I was ready to settle down with the woman of my dreams. The only other woman who had my last name was my mama. Now it was time to change that.

I parked half a block down from Colay's just like we did the day before. We watched as the last of the stragglers left the house and everything became quiet. One by one all the lights started turning off inside the crib. The last one to go out was the one closest to the left side of the house. From what Marina told us, that was Colay's room. We noticed that after two in the morning nobody came in or out. That fit shit just perfect for us.

We stayed only forty-five minutes more to be sure we didn't miss anything. The silence from earlier was still lingering between us. I was thinking of ways to get rid of DJ without any extra backlash from Amon. I didn't want no beef but if it came down to it, then so be it.

We pulled in our complex and parked. I gave my brother some dap and promised to see him the following day.

I crept in the house quietly making sure not to wake anyone. I didn't even bother to turn on any lights. All I wanted to do was get naked and get my freak on. Yeah I know I know, we been fucking like crazy right? Well I had a beautiful ass woman I couldn't get enough of so sue me. If you had a woman as irresistible as Marina shiiiiiid! You'd wanna keep her satisfied too! I stripped out my clothes and slid under the blanket next to my baby.

I moved her hair from her neck and started placing light kisses all over her. I reached to pull her closer to me and realized she was butt ass naked. That woman just knew the way to my heart. I gently rolled her on her back. I kissed down her body stopping at her breasts to give them each of them equal attention. Then I placed a trail of kisses down her belly to her thighs. I spread her legs and went to town. I was feasting on my baby's juicy love box when I heard that gasp.

That gasp was the sexiest thing coming from her. I always loved waking her up and that gasp was always how I knew that she felt me. She woke up trying to wiggle around but I had a firm grip on her. She started grinding against my face as I held her tightly in place. She was moaning and calling my name. I felt her legs tighten up so I knew she was about to cum.

Before she could fully finish her orgasm I moved in and buried myself deep inside of her. We had this chemistry that was always amplified by one hundred when we were sexing.

That night was different though. I wanted to make love to her soul. I wanted her to know that I truly loved her with everything in me. I slow stroked her to her next orgasm. I felt her grip on me but I didn't stop. She was moaning and whispering in my ear.

If she didn't stop saying all that sexy shit in my ear I was gonna bust early. I didn't want to but I felt it coming. I pulled out and bust my nut all on her stomach. She looked at me like a madwoman but said nothing. I grabbed my beater from the side of the bed and wiped her off. Before I could jump back in her, she pushed me down and straddled me. I felt her ease down on my dick and I was in heaven.

That pussy was made for me and that's just what I told her as she rode me. Marina rode me nice and slow. I was in love with that woman in so many ways. I made sure to show her the way I caressed her body.

Marina rode me until she had two more orgasms and then we switched positions. I smacked her ass and told her to set that shit up for me. She did as she was told and set that ass up real nice for me.

I slid into her tight pussy with a deep moan. I started stroking her, slow at first then faster. Pretty soon she was throwing it back at me. I was loving that shit. I had a nice grip on her ass with one hand and her hair in the other hand. I felt her pussy muscles start to contract so I knew she was about to cum. Shit, I was getting ready to cum with her. She continued to throw it back at me while I was beating it up and then we both came simultaneously. I pulled out of her and lay next to her exhausted.

Marina moved over to me so she could lay on my chest. Within minutes she was snoring lightly. I felt good about myself because that meant I hit her with that knockout dick. I chuckled to myself as I thought that. I looked up to notice the light starting to creep in from the blinds and decided to get a couple hours of shut eye. Tonight was the night and I had to on point.

Marina

Damn, Timothy came home and put it on me and put me right back to sleep. It was the best sex session we had ever had by far. Our relationship was getting stronger by the day and I couldn't have been more happy.

Still feeling groggy at seven the next morning, Timothy let me sleep while he got the kids breakfast. They were spending the day at Cheryl's while I went out looking for a new spot. There was no way I was going to keep my family in those damn apartments after we murked Colay.

"So what are you gonna do today?" Timothy asked as he served me hotcakes and sausage in the bed.

"I have to do a little shopping," I replied with the half-truth. "I need to keep myself busy so I won't keep thinking about tonight."

"You don't have shit to worry about Marina!"

The way Timothy looked at me let me know that he was serious. I started shoving food in my mouth before I said something stupid.

"You know that don't you?"

I nodded yes so I wouldn't speak with my mouth full.

"All this shit I'm doing to make sure you and the kids are safe. He already made it clear that he was gonna come back for my life, so this is the only way."

"I know and I'm not trippin'. Trust me."

Timothy kissed my cheek and let me finish my meal in peace. He let me know that he might not see me until afterwards. That's when I knew I had to come up with something because I didn't even feel safe bringing my kids back up in there after Colay was dead. Everyone knew where I lived and if anything went wrong that would be the first place they would come and look.

"Well, don't come back here when you finish. Meet me at Cheryl's place."

"Cool, I didn't even think about all that," he admitted. "That's why I love you so much!"

"Why?"

"Because you have brains and beauty!"

I laughed his ass right on out the door. I needed time to take care of what I needed to before he got done with his deed.

After getting dressed and sending the kids over Cheryl's, I pulled out all the listings that I had jotted down. I had them in order according to location. The first one was over thirty minutes away.

"I want this house!" I thought the moment I pulled up in front of the two story modern house with a pool.

The real estate agent was already inside. She saw how excited I was and began the tour right away. When we were finished, she started with the questions.

"How soon were you looking to buy?"

"Today if possible."

"Well you know it could take up to thirty days to close the deal," she informed me.

"I definitely don't have that kind of time," I smirked. "But I have 40 thousand to put down on it."

The agent's eyes lit up by the amount of cash I was referring to. That must have gotten her thinking cap going because within minutes she had a great suggestion.

"Well, what I can do is work up a quick loan approval. If that goes through, then I can call the owner and see if he can work out a deal to get you in here today."

"For real?"

"Yes. I see the determination in your eyes and I really want to help."

I knew that was bullshit. What she really wanted was that fucking commission. But I was cool with that if she could get the ball rolling soon.

"Give me a couple of hours and I'll call you with a definite answer," she assured on our way out to the turnaround driveway. "I know the owner personally so I'm almost positive that he will work with you. Just be ready."

She waved and jumped into her big body Benz and peeled out. I waited until she was out of sight before I began screaming with excitement.

I had never owned anything in my life except for my three year old van and that was a big accomplishment for me. So to step my game up and be able to buy a house was unbelievable.

Feeling happy I kept my job, I knew I would need it when it came to the paperwork. I didn't want the authorities to question where I got such a big lump sum of money to buy a damn house. That along with me always keeping a proper savings account would ensure that I was very capable of buying my own shit. As hard as I had worked all my life, I was to the point where I wish a motherfucker would try to question me about my finances.

I had to get Cheryl on the line to share the great news. When she didn't answer, I knew it was a sign to wait until afterwards to tell her.

Since we lived right next door to one another, I knew that there was no way to sneak my shit out without her noticing.

"Damn I am smart," I thought out loud as I walked to Cheryl's door.

"Hey Marina, you back so soon?"

"Yeah, I'm not done yet though."

"So what's up then?"

"I wanted to bring you some money to take the kids to the movies. You can use my van if I can use your Honda."

"Cool, they're tired of being up in that room playin' the damn game anyway."

Shit was moving smoothly and I was getting anxious. We quickly exchanged sets of keys and I was out. I headed inside my apartment to start packing my necessities. By the time I got through with the kids rooms, my cell was ringing. It was the real estate agent.

"Great news Marina!"

I didn't let her get it out good before I started yelling. She waited for me to stop to tell me that she would meet me at the house with the paperwork by five. The timing was perfect.

Rushing to get a U-Haul, I jammed as much stuff as I could inside. I left my run down furniture and took only our personal items.

I made it to the new house, signed the documents, unloaded my things and returned the truck all by nine o'clock that evening. Then I went straight back to Cheryl's. I needed a drink. In fact, I needed to see my man...

I hadn't heard a peep from him but I hadn't expected to. That didn't keep my nerves from being wrecked though. I was still worried...

"Cheryl let me get up out of here before Timothy makes it back," I blurted out into the quiet living room.

My friend was over on the sofa knocked the hell out. I went and got a blanket and threw it over her. I used the bathroom and made my way out the door, locking it behind me.

The crisp night air made me gasp as I bundled up underneath my thin jacket. That's when I felt someone come up behind me. Before I could yell, my mouth was covered with some strange smelling rag.

That was the last thing I remembered before waking up in a familiar room...

Timothy

Marina was on some sneaky shit but I wasn't worried. I knew that whatever she was doing, she did it with a purpose. If anything, she was setting us up for the next phase in our life. She made a point when she said she didn't want no shit brought back to her house if something went wrong. I didn't even factor in that possibility.

I had to focus. It was getting down to that time. I didn't need any distractions so I pushed everything to the side. I went over the plan in my head about a thousand times. Me and Terrell had already scoped out Colay's spot enough to know what was going on outside. With the info that Marina gave us about the inside of the house, shit was all good. All I had was time now.

I laid in bed at my mama's house as I thought of how I wanted to murk this nigga. Was I gonna beat him up first? Would I just put two in his head right away? Nah! I think I'll torture his ass for a little bit before I kill him. It would serve his bitch ass right though after all he put Marina through. When she told me everything I wanted to kill his ass right then and there. It wasn't until he shot me that it ended up being really personal.

I ended up dozing off but about one AM I awoke to the sound of my cell phone ringing. Not bothering to check who it was, I answered.

"Yo."

"Babe....BABE!"

"Marina? Babe are you ok?"

"Ha ha ha....nigga you sound like a bitch! Babe are you ok? Lame ass nigga. Fuck outta here! THIS MY BITCH! Always has been and always will be. If I can't have her then nobody fucking will. That's my word. Come find me bitch nigga!"

With that Colay's bitch ass hung up on me. I frantically called Marina's phone back only to the voicemail each time. FUCK! Shit just got too fucking real. I dialed Terrell's number as I got dressed. He answered on the third ring.

"Calm yo anxious ass down boe. Shit ain't posed to go do-"

"Boe he got my girl! That bitch ass nigga got my fucking woman! Imma kill his ass fo sho when I get my hands on him!"

"Hold up, what? Awww hell nah. I'm on my way."

After hanging up with Terrell I laced my boots up, grabbed my heat and hoodie and went outside to wait on him. He pulled up ten minutes later. I hopped in the car and no words were exchanged. I was on a mission to get my girl back.

On the outside I was cool, calm and collected but on the inside I was fuming mad. I couldn't believe that nigga pulled that shit on me. Hadn't he done enough to Marina? I couldn't fall apart though. I had to keep my composure in order to get my woman back safely. I needed to concentrate because not only would I have to take Colay's life but I would have to save Marina's.

We pulled up on his block just like we'd done previous times before and saw no activity. There was only one light on in the entire house; Colay's room. I wanted to storm in there with guns blazing but I knew if I did that then there was a chance he'd kill Marina. Naw it was strategy time. We had to make sure that when we went in that joint, we both came back out alive.

We both got out the car and headed to the house. I crept around the back while Terrell crept around the side. He found a small window that was unlocked. We decided that would be our point of entry. We knew what being a criminal was all-about so breaking into a house was easy. We sat in the dark for about ten minutes listening to see if there was anyone inside besides Colay.

I heard muffled voices coming from the front of the house so I moved closer without making a noise. I hoped like hell that he was alone. I didn't want there to be anymore shit than necessary to pop off. The closer I got, the better I could hear the conversation. It was Colay and some dude talking.

I couldn't make out the voice but something told me to get a look at him. I was able to maneuver in the dark to a spot where I could see what was going on. I saw Marina with her hands and feet tied up. It took everything in me not to just hop up and start shooting. That wasn't the worst part though. The other nigga talking was none other than DJ's slick ass! I already knew I didn't like his ass and with what Tina told us the other day, I knew we'd have a problem with him. I sat there ear hustling for a minute.

"Good job on getting Marina to trust you DJ. I knew she would be a gullible bitch for a pretty nigga."

"Hey I ain't no pretty nigga, you just hating. I just wanted my piece and I'm out."

"Well go ahead and have at it my nigga. She got some good pussy too! Why you think we got all them kids?"

That shit made my blood boil! I knew he wasn't about to do what I thought but when he pulled her from the chair and laid her on the floor, he confirmed that for me. It was time to move. I signaled to Terrell to follow my lead. As we crept through the darkened hallway towards them niggas I heard Marina start to cry and talk at the same time.

"No no no! DJ please don't do this! Why man why? I thought we were cool."

"Money talks and bullshit walks bitch. Now shut the fuck up and let me get that pussy from you."

I heard a struggle and then Marina screamed out. Colay just stood back and laughed at the shit like it was funny. Before they could realize what happened, I had snatched Colay's ass up and put my gun to his head. DJ stopped what he was doing to see Terrell standing over him with a gun.

"Go ahead nigga. Give me another fucking reason boe!"

That nigga just laughed at us. Terrell hit him across the head with the butt of his gun. It only made the nigga laugh even harder. The shit wasn't a fucking game! I gave Terrell a look and he started pistol whipping DJ. The nigga finally passed out after the beating Terrell put on him.

Terrell rushed to Marina to untie her. I still had Colay hemmed up and he was shaking like a little bitch. He had even pissed on himself. He disgusted me in the worse way. I hit him in the back of the head with my gun and he crumpled to the floor. I really wanted to let loose into his ass but I decided to let my woman do it.

As soon as she was free, she ran over to where Colay was laying and just started stomping on him. She yelled obscenities as tears fell from her eyes. I didn't want to stop her but felt it was necessary to get back to business. I pulled

Colay up off the floor and sat him in the same chair that he had Marina in. I made sure he was tied up nice and tight before I woke his ass up. Terrell had DJ tied up as well but he left him on the floor where he was at.

Marina threw a cup of cold water in Colay's face to wake him up. When his eyes popped open he looked at Marina with a bewildered look on his face. His eyes darted around the room at all of us. When he saw DJ tied up, his eyes really got big. I just handed Marina my gun and stepped back. I saw a tear slide down his face before Marina went the fuck off on him.

"So that's what the fuck we do now Colay? 12 fucking years I was with you. I dealt with all your hoes, drama and bullshit for all them years and when I decide to move on, you come for me? BITCH NIGGA I DIDN'T SEND FOR YOU! You shoot my man, you get another weak nigga to kidnap me and then you was about to let him rape me. Tell me something, did you even think about our kids in all this? I know you didn't because if you did then you would realize what you would've taken away from them. You ain't shit and this ends tonight!"

Marina walked over to Colay's crybaby ass, pressed the gun under his chin and fired a single shot. Colay's brains were splattered everywhere. She didn't flinch or anything when she pulled the trigger. I loved her gangsta! Now wasn't the time to get my dick hard though even though she just did that shit. I took the smoking gun from Marina's hand and led her into the next room. I gave her specific instructions to stay put.

Terrell drug DJ into the same room Marina was in and then came to help me. I had to shoot Amon a text from a number he was familiar with so I used Marina's phone. Within minutes he was calling. I quickly explained what went down, in code of course, and he assured me that he had a team on the way. He also instructed me to keep DJ alive. As soon as I ended the conversation we heard a scuffling noise coming from the next room.

We both ran to see what was going on but by the time we got into the room, Marina was laying on the floor covered in blood. I noticed an open window too but I didn't care about that shit right then and there. My focus was on Marina. I instructed Terrell to go get the car. As soon as he got to the door the crew was there coming in. We left them to their business while we attended to ours.

Terrell did almost a hundred on his way to the hospital. I sat in the backseat cradling Marina's head in my hands. I had never cried over a woman before and I wasn't ashamed to be crying now. I loved that woman with everything in me. There was no way in hell I was going to lose her. We pulled up at the emergency entrance and Terrell jumped out the car and ran in. He was followed back out by a few nurses and a doctor. I handed them my baby before I passed out.

Marina

My head was spinning when I came out of my daze. I was tied up and in one of the rooms at the house where Colay was staying.   DJ was the one that snatched me up.

"Bitch you tried to play me close. I told you to stick to the plan and ya ass wanna play funny and shit!"

As his hands caressed my breasts, Colay walked in and began to flip out on me. I could handle the name calling, but when he commenced to whooping my ass like I stole something, I thought I was going to die.

After what seemed like hours passed, I was exhausted of being tortured. Right when I thought I was going to lose it, Timothy and his brother came to save the day. So I thought...

Yes, I did get the pleasure of killing my ex-husband, but what I didn't expect was DJ coming for me like he did. I was definitely caught off guard.

The first sharp pain was to my side. The piercing left me with a shortness of breath. When I turned around to grab DJ's hand, I noticed the butterfly knife. He twirled it around as if he was a pro with it. We instantly began to tussle for the blade. That's when he punctured my shoulder, close to my neck. Blood began to squirt everywhere and I had to let him loose from my grip in order to control the bleeding.

"I told you that you didn't have a fuckin' clue who you were fuckin' with!" DJ spat before hopping out of the window.

My injuries made it impossible for me to scream. I just laid my head back, clinched my wound and began to shake violently before passing out again...

A Cold chill engulfed my body as I gasped for air. The tubes down my throat caused me to panic. Momentarily, I was disorientated but that was quickly balanced once I looked up and saw my man.

"Baby, damn, baby, damn you scared the shit out of me!"

Timothy grabbed my hand and squeezed it as he bent down and kissed my cheek. I let the tears roll as I began to remember the horrific outcome of our plan to take out Colay. I not only had murdered my kid's father, I had damn near died at the hands of DJ.

Anxiety kicked in and sent me into a panic as I thought about them not being able to 'cleanup' behind our 'fuck up'.

"What's up?"

Timothy seemed to start stressing and was about to call for the doctor, but Terrell motioned him to wait. He stepped close to the bed and whispered.

"Don't worry about shit. Stick to the story. We handled everything."

Just as he backed away, the emergency physician and the local authorities were walking in. I played like I was still out of it and let Timothy and Terrell answer all the questions.

"We're going to need you two to come down to the precinct to answer a few questions."

"Seriously?" Timothy barked. "My girl is laying here fighting for her fuckin' life and you want me to leave? Can't you just ask me that shit right here?"

I wanted to yell at him and tell him to shut the fuck up and cooperate. We didn't need any additional heat on our back. Luckily, Terrell intervened at just the right time.

"Naw boe, let's get on with this so they can find the dirty motherfucker that did this shit."

The calmness in his voice led me to believe that his brother was going to listen to him. He attempted to argue for a second, but Terrell wasn't having the shit.

"Well could you at least have a security guard or something at her door?"

I heard one of the policemen chuckle. I wanted to open my eyes so fucking bad, just to peek, but I knew that my mouth would open right behind it and I couldn't say shit. I still had the fucking tubes down my throat.

"Ain't shit funny fat boy!" Timothy snapped.

"Alright now let's settle down in here! I have a patient to tend to! Can we show just a little respect for her?" The doctor spat. "Now I'm going to need you to take that in the hallway."

"I do apologize," the female cop spoke. "We're going to take them downtown. I will get hospital security up here as soon as we can."

I felt Timothy press his warm lips on my forehead. He told me to sit tight and that he would be right back. I didn't make a move. I was completely still.

"I love you baby."

The urge to tell him back was overwhelming me. I could feel the liquid filling my tightly shut lids. I suppressed them for as long as I could, but just as I heard the door close I felt the warm wetness creep down my face.

As the doctor began to take my vitals, he must have noticed my tears because I felt a tissue wipe them away. I allowed it without moving a muscle. I still laid there as still as possible. I needed them to think that I was still out of it until I was able to talk to Timothy first. I wasn't saying shit until then.

I waited for a few minutes after the doctor to leave to open my eyes, but right when I did I saw someone coming back in. Figuring he forgot to check something, I went back to playing 'comatose'. That was up until I felt the tube being shoved deeper into my esophagus.

My eyes bucked wide open as I saw DJ staring down at me. He didn't speak right away. He was too busy moving the phone and call button out of my reach.

"I see ya wide awake now huh bitch?" DJ whispered. "I could kill you right the fuck now. But what fun would that be if I couldn't fuck you first?"

Digging my nails into his skin, I tried my damnedest to pry his hands from my mouth. The tube was doing some serious damage and I wasn't sure how much more I could take.

"I shoulda just fucked you back at the house, but that buster ass Colay fucked all that up. The thing about me is, I'm a determined motherfucker that doesn't stop until he gets what he wants."

Shaking my head no and tapping the rail, I let him know I had enough. He just looked at me and smacked his lips.

"Thing is, I'm not gonna fuck you right now, but I am gonna fuck you. I saw you kill ya ex-husband in cold blood and I will get all you locked the fuck up quicker than you can blink." DJ whispered as he let go of my mouth.

Snatching the tube out as quickly as I could, I began choking hysterically. Instead of getting me some help, he exposed his hand. He told me that he knew where my new house was. He even recited the fucking address.

"I know you haven't told ya dude that shit, so that's gonna be our little secret until I get what I want from you. And, if you think this is just about me gettin' some pussy from you ya dead ass wrong. That shit is just a bonus baby."

Before I could catch my breath, he was gone. I couldn't get up and get to the nurse's button fast enough to press it. I couldn't yell and I was still hooked up to the IV but that didn't stop me from trying to get the hell out of that bed and get someone to come and help me.

"What's wrong?" the nurse asked in a panic. "Let me get you back in this bed.

Waving her off, I tried to tell her what happened without using words. Every time I tried to speak I began to cough. She must have thought I was tripping because before I knew it two more staff members were coming to sedate me.

Shaking my head 'no' I placed my hand in the way so they couldn't inject my arm.

"Turn her over and hold her down!" the doctor ordered as he injected a warm fluid into my right ass cheek.

My fight was over quickly and that medicine sent me straight to the land of 'feel-good'. I was out like a light.

I don't know how long I was asleep but when I came to, Timothy was all up in my grill smiling. I wish I could have smiled back at him but the only thing I could think about was my little visit from DJ. His threat was stuck in my mind. I wasn't ready to tell. Not just yet…

"How are you feeling baby?"

Looking over to the counter, I motioned for him to give me a glass of water. It took him several guesses before he figured out what the hell I wanted.

Taking a few gulps, I tried to speak.

"What did the police say?" I whispered.

"I'll explain all that when we get you up out of here. I don't know if that bitch ass nigga DJ is bold enough to try us up in here."

If he only knew what had already happened. I couldn't hold it in much longer, but I didn't have much of a choice. I didn't want to risk the chance of him flying off the handle in the hospital. Considering the circumstances, I thought it was best to tell him once I was released.

"Who has the kids?"

"They're with my mother. I didn't think it was safe to leave them at Cheryl's. It's just too close to the house."

"DJ knows where your mother lives!" I replied in a hoarse tone.

My nerves were becoming more wrecked by the second and I didn't know what to do. Even though Timothy stood there and tried his best to convince me that they were safe and all of his brothers were there with them, I still didn't feel any better. I needed to know for sure. I had to get the fuck out of there and get to my babies.

"Did they say when I could leave?"

"Yeah, they said in a few days."

That wasn't fast enough! I couldn't wait...

Timothy

When I got back to the hospital I was told that Marina had an episode. Apparently she woke up, spazzed out and pulled the tube out her throat. The doctor had to sedate her. When I walked into her room she was sleeping peacefully so I just sat there looking at her gorgeous face. She was so damn beautiful to me. She started to stir after about an hour so I got up and stood next to her bed.

I was cheesing all in her face when she came to. She was motioning for something and it took me a few tries before I figured out that she wanted some water. I watched her as she sucked down the clear cold liquid before she could speak to me. She spoke in a whisper and I answered each of her questions. She was scared that something would happen to her kids.

I assured her that they were safe with my mother and all my brothers before she relaxed a little. She really wasn't trying to hear that she had to stay a few days but I was more worried about her getting better. We had been through the most already in the small amount of time we had been together. I just wanted to push past all this bullshit and live our life quietly. I stayed until visiting hours were over before I left. I had some business to handle.

I made a call to Tina to see if she could come up with anything that could lead me to DJ. We wouldn't be safe until I got rid of that crazy bastard. If she could get me a lead on him then I'd make sure to hunt his ass down and slaughter him. I drove towards Tina's house but not before hitting up Terrell. So far my brother had been my keeper. I didn't want to make a move without him.

Terrell was at Tina's house when I got there. Tina was tapping away at the computer when he let me in. I would definitely have to hit her off with a few dollars when all this was done. She was proving to be an asset to us lately. I would definitely talk to Terrell about keeping her on our team. I chopped it up with my brother before Tina came over to us.

"Here's what ya asked for boss but I got something else I wanna show you. It's a video."

"Well show me then."

I followed Tina back to her computer while I looked over the few sheets of paper she gave me. As my eyes darted back and forth between the papers and her computer screen, my eyes bucked. On her screen was DJ in the hospital right after we left. She played us a video feed that showed us leaving with the cops and not too long after, DJ was going in to Marina's room.

We weren't able to see what happened in the room because there were no cameras in there but he exited about fifteen minutes later. Obviously Marina was ok because I had just left her. So why would the doctor and nurses rush into her room?

I was livid. I wondered why Marina didn't tell me about his visit. Maybe he didn't do anything to her but I didn't put shit past dude.

After watching the video and reading everything on the papers Tina gave me, I now had an idea on how to get that asshole. My best bet was to use Marina as bait, but I didn't think she'd mind. She wanted his ass bad as I did. I gave her Colay but DJ was mine. I was gonna enjoy putting a bullet in his head. I left to go check on Marina's kids before I put my plan together.

The next morning I helped my mama get the kids together and off to school. The smaller ones that didn't go to school yet stayed with her at home and I left my two younger brothers watching over all of them. I knew they'd be safe there.

Once everyone was situated I made my way to the hospital. I was anxious to run this plan down to Marina to see what she thought about it. Plus I wanted to know about the shit that happened with DJ. I didn't want to upset her so I was going to choose my words wisely.

I walked in Marina's room to see her sitting up and watching TV. I was glad my baby was getting better. I kissed her lips before telling her what I found out.

"Hey babe I wanna run something by you."

"Does it involve me getting out of here?"

"Yeah but it might get a little dangerous."

"I don't give a shit as long as I get out of here. So what's the tea?"

"Well DJ has this weird ass obsession with you right? And I know that he came to see you yesterday after we left."

"Babe I can explain."

"Don't worry about it. Check this out though. Tina found out that Amon is now looking for DJ. Come to find out, he was in on the shit with Colay when it came to taking Amon's money. That was the reason he was at the house that night. He convinced Colay to let him get close to you so he could kidnap you and do what he wanted. Colay agreed to let him have you in exchange for him getting to keep the money. DJ wants you and won't stop at nothing to get you."

"Ok so what do you need me to do babe?"

"We have to find a way to get DJ to come to us and you're the perfect person to do it. We just need a place where we'd be able to take cover in so nothing else happens to you."

"I know just the place babe. Now get me the hell out of here so I can show you."

I left the room to go speak to a doctor about Marina's release. I knew it was too soon for her to leave the hospital but we needed to get DJ out the way. I couldn't keep living and having to look over my shoulder. I wouldn't let Marina or the kids do it either.

After much negotiating and promising, I got the doctor to release Marina. I made my way back to her room to give her the good news.

"Let's blow this popsicle joint babe."

"Good cause I'm ready."

I helped Marina get dressed so we could get the ball rolling. As I left to get the car, the nurse wheeled Marina downstairs. I was anxious as hell to get DJ. That was gonna be his last night breathing if I had anything to do with it.

Pulling right up to the front entrance, I helped Marina into the car. She directed me down All American Freeway and told me to get off at the Santa Fe exit.

Veering off onto the road, I followed her directions. Soon after, we were driving down NC-87 towards Sanford. I wanted to ask where we were going but I decided against it.

I was just gonna trust where she was taking me. We drove into Harnett County and when we got to Buffalo Lake Road we made a right turn and then another right turn down Winding Ridge. We drove for about half a mile down the street made of loose gravel before she asked me to slow down. She told me to make the left turn into the driveway of this big house.

I did as she instructed and when I parked, she hopped out the car.

"Slow ya ass down baby!" I whispered as I got out slowly behind her and followed closely.

It shocked the shit out of me when she pulled out a set of keys. I looked at her strangely but she nodded at me to follow her inside. I walked into a big beautiful entranceway. It led into a huge living room with a bay window and sliding glass doors to the patio.

I trailed behind her as she showed me each room. The kitchen was royal blue and white with stainless steel appliances and more than enough space for her to move around in. Next, she led me upstairs where she showed me the four bedrooms. I realized that the house we were in was her dream home. Even though it was short a few bedrooms, it was still the place she described to me when we were talking one night.

I couldn't have her lure DJ there. Not if that was her dream. I didn't want her to have any bad memories there. I had to say something so I did.

"Babe this is the house you've dreamt of. I can't have that psycho here. I don't want you to have any bad memories up in here."

"Don't worry about him making it to the house because he's only gonna get as far as the neighborhood. Once we catch him coming in we'll take him into the woods. If you haven't noticed, in the back of this house is nothing but woods. A person could get lost in there which is exactly what we need him to do. You catch my drift?"

"Yeah I'm following your lead babe."

We shared a few more ideas as she led me around the rest of the house. That joint had everything; even a basement. That right there was definitely gonna be my man cave. I laughed at the thought. That house was gonna hold great memories for us but it wouldn't be right if we didn't move into together as husband and wife. Once we took care of DJ, I was gonna propose to Marina. I wanted to give her something no other woman would ever get from me; my last name.

Marina

As Timothy drove me down the road that led to our new home, I watched the perimeter closely. I took him a roundabout way just so that I could make sure that DJ wasn't lurking around. I just prayed that he didn't find out that I was released from the hospital so soon.

Timothy was feeling bad about doing the shit up in the house, so I had to guarantee him that he wouldn't make it to the door. I sort of had a plan, but it was still in the works.

"Can you have Terrell take the kids and meet us at the Marriott on the east side?" I requested as I set the alarm on the house before leaving.

I needed for everyone to be together when we took DJ out. He was sneaky and I was definitely not going to underestimate his ass. He knew everywhere I frequented, including Timothy's mother's house. I figured that we at least had an hour or so before he would find out that he didn't know where I was. We had to hurry.

It took us no time to check the kids in.

"Mom, why are we coming here?" Lupe asked.

"It's like a mini vacation. They have an indoor pool so I'll take you guys swimming! We can even order room service!" Cheryl explained with enthusiasm.

"What's room service?" Lupe continued to question.

"Now I've only seen it on the movies, so this is gonna be fun for auntie Cheryl too," she laughed. "It's when we pick up the phone and tell them what we want and they bring it to us, for free!"

We all busted out laughing! Cheryl was a lifesaver and I was grateful to have her in my circle. I wouldn't trade her for the world.

After we got the kids settled in, Timothy grabbed my hand and began to pull me.

"What's up baby? Where are we going?"

Revealing an additional key card, he let me know that we had our own suite. I couldn't believe it. In the middle of all the confusion, Timothy found a way for us to have some quality time.

Kissing the kids goodbye, I let them know that I would still be in the same building, but on a different floor.

"Why didn't you get a room next door?" I quizzed as we stepped out into the hallway.

"You think I wanted the kids to hear ya head knockin' on the headboard?" Timothy clowned as he ran away from me.

"You know that shit ain't fair right?" I yelled as I eased toward the elevator. "You are so fuckin' lucky that I can't chase you right now! I'm a little sore. I think I need a pain pill or some shit."

"So ya head can be all fucked up when it's time to go?" he snapped. "If you ain't feelin' up to this shit, we can put it on hold or I'll just handle it a different way!"

Not wanting to argue, I shut his ass up by pulling him to me and placing a sensual kiss on his unsuspecting lips. I caught him off guard but he rolled with that shit. My injuries were not going to stop me from getting some.

Coming at him aggressively as soon as he unlocked the door, he responded accordingly. Using his foot, he gently kicked the door to ensure its closure.

"Baby, are you sure about this?" Timothy whispered as he fell back onto the bed thanks to the light shove I administered to his chest.

"Oh, I'm sure," I guaranteed.

As I began to do a slow grind on top of him, I felt his nature rise. Staring down at him to see his reaction, we locked eyes. His smile lit me up in the wildest ways, and those three special words topped the shit off.

"I love you."

My heart fluttered and I giggled as I continued to wind my hips against his hardness. My wounds were hurting so bad, but not enough for me to stop. I had to have him.

"I love you too baby," I grunted.

"See, ya ass is in pain! Look at you! You still want some!" Timothy teased as he gently reversed our position. "Relax! I'll make sure you get yours and then some."

I wanted some but I knew with the skills my man possessed, it was about to be on and crackin'! I lifted my knees up, let Timothy slide my pants and undies off and he went to town. Damn....

Shit was going so good. I was just about to get my second one when my cell began to ring. I ignored it. I needed no interruptions. Timothy tried to lift his head but I tightened my thighs and pumped a good three more times before I let loose.

"Whoa, I'm so sorry baby," I apologized with a slight giggle. "I just had to get that last one! Damn baby! You just be havin' my ass goin'!"

As I reached for him to cuddle, he reached for my cell. He really knew how to fuck up a moment. I clinched the pillow and held it tightly so that I could savor the incredible feeling that my man had just so graciously given me. I couldn't be mad.

"It's DJ!" Timothy whispered. "You ready to talk?"

Feeling that I didn't have too much of a choice, I sat up and took the phone from him. I pressed the talk button and listened to DJ yelling.

"You think you real slick right about now don't you Marina? I'll find you! The first place I'm going to is ya' man's mom's house. If you're not waiting outside, I'm gonna start fucking shit up! I'm gonna go to ya homegirl's Cheryl's house next and do the same shit. I'm not talking about busting out windows and shit. I'm talking about bringing the fuckin' rain! What cha' know about that? Huh Marina? What cha' know about that?"

After taking a deep breath, I began to play the role. I lied and told him that I had to sneak out of the hospital so that Timothy didn't know about me meeting up with him. I explained how him and Terrell were out to get him.

"We have to meet on the low."

"Why? That nigga don't know shit about the house do he? Why we can't just meet there?"

"We can, but I can't drive and you can't come and get me. I don't want to take the chance of Timothy finding out." I went on sounding as convincing as I possibly could.

It wasn't as easy as I thought. DJ brought up how he stabbed me. He knew I wanted revenge and he didn't trust me at all. I needed to gain that in order for the plan to work.

"What is it exactly that you want from me DJ?" I snapped getting frustrated. "Do you want to kill me?"

"I want to fuck you, then I'll decide!"

Closing my eyes, I shook my head in disgust. I couldn't believe the country ass shit that he was letting fly out of his trap. If I was in front of him, I would have shut his ass up permanently. I wanted his death by my hands so bad that I could taste the shit!

"So how the fuck am I supposed to take that shit DJ?" I spat getting bold.

DJ liked that shit. That seemed to turn him on more, so I ran with it.

"I'm all with fuckin' the shit outta you but if you talkin' crazy then we may as well handle the shit on the streets!"

"Damn boo, like that?" DJ chuckled.

"Hell fuckin' yeah! Just like that!" I stated firmly.

"Well then it looks like we gotta a date to fuck then! That's what the fuck I'm talkin' about baby."

Now DJ's tone had calmed down a great deal, but Timothy's attitude was shifting. He gave me the dirtiest look and when he did, I shrugged my shoulders and whispered to him.

"What was I supposed to say?"

Timothy waved me off and nodded his head for me to continue. Shit was stressful enough without him breathing over my damn shoulder. Hell, I didn't like talking to DJ like that, let alone wanting to fuck him. He was handsome on the outside and all but he was crazy as hell on the inside. That was a crazy I had to dead!

After five more minutes of bullshit I persuaded DJ to meet me at the house. I didn't even have to tell him to park his car down the road. He let me know he was going to do that shit anyway. He didn't trust me and I definitely didn't trust him.

"So when are you coming?"

"It's late and how are you gonna get there? I thought you couldn't drive?"

"I can have Cheryl take me in her car."

"Well, have her bring you to meet me and I'll drive from there." DJ demanded.

"I don't want her all in my business like that! And she's not gonna just drop me off somewhere with everything that's goin' on!"

"Damn, you gotta point."

Hurrying him up off the phone, I let him know that I needed to call Cheryl and hook things up.

"I will call you back when I know."

"No, you better be hittin' my fuckin' line in the next thirty minutes Marina! Don't play with me! I hate for shit to get ugly!"

"Seriously DJ?" Are you back on that shit?" I checked his ass. "If ya gonna be acting stupid and shit fuck it!"

"Naw, naw, just call me right back!"

We hung up and Timothy was all in my face fussing about me talking to DJ that long and not getting anything accomplished.

"I thought you had a fuckin' plan Marina!" he snapped. "I'm gonna ask you this shit one more time! Do I need to handle this shit myself?"

Sitting there feeling stupid, I let him know that I had everything under control. I guess he didn't believe me, because he called his brother to the room to come up with a plan of his own...

Timothy

Lord knows I loved Marina to death but I felt like she was testing me. She was going into the shit with DJ blindly. I needed no mistakes to be made because if that nigga hurt her again or even killed her, I was going to make it my goal in life to execute his ass.

It pissed me off that the nigga was talking about fucking my girl. I knew she wasn't gonna do it but damn! It took everything in me not to take the phone and go off on his ass.

Once I called Terrell, him and Cheryl rushed up to our floor after getting my mama to sit with the kids. She was in the hotel too. We all had separate rooms just in case some shit happened. I opened the door for them while Marina was lying on the bed, clearly her injuries were bothering her. That made me not even want to let her out of my sight, but she was our only way of getting close to DJ.

"So this bitch nigga just called Marina's phone talking all reckless and shit. I swear I wanna body his ass right the fuck now!"

"Calm down boe. Now tell me what happened."

I took a few deep breaths and told Terrell about the conversation. While I was explaining to him about the half ass plan Marina had, something went off in my head. I got it! I excitedly began to tell Terrell my idea. The more I enlightened him, the more hyped he got. Cheryl and Marina noticed our animated talking so they came over to join us.

Marina was in obvious pain. As much as I wanted her to sit out on this one, I knew she wouldn't. I explained to the women that Terrell and I would leave now to go to the new house. Cheryl was to take Marina to meet DJ as planned and once she did so, she was to call me or Terrell about the drop-off. Terrell agreed to post up at the top of the street to check where they would park.

Everyone thought it was best that since I had such animosity towards DJ, I should be the one posted closest to the house. They didn't wanna take any chances with me killing him before making sure that Marina was ok. We didn't wanna make a move before we needed to.

Terrell and I left right away so we could be in place. I instructed Marina to make the call after I left because I couldn't stomach her talking to that nigga again.

My brother and I headed to the house. We arrived there and immediately got in position and waited. Cheryl texted Terrell when they were on their way to the drop spot. She was supposed to hit us up after she left Marina with DJ but she hadn't yet.

Thirty minutes went by before we got anymore contact from Cheryl. Apparently when she dropped Marina off to DJ, he took her car keys and tossed them into the wooded area off the side on NC-87. She said he snatched Marina up like a mad man, tossed her in the car and drove off like a bat out of hell.

FUCK! Shit wasn't going as planned and I was pissed. That crazy muthafucka could have been anywhere with my girl. It was time for Plan B.

I hit Terrell up and let him know what was going on. We both knew that DJ knew where the new house was. We also knew that his ass was crazy and sick enough to try to taint Marina's spirit by doing some shit in that house. I wasn't having that shit.

I crept down the block towards the crib when I saw lights approaching. A dark colored car pulled into the driveway and the engine cut off. I watched silently as DJ pulled an unconscious Marina out the car. It took all the restraint in me not to shoot his ass on site. He tossed Marina over his shoulder like it was nothing and started towards the house.

Before he could get the door open, a car came flying up the street and pulled into the driveway smashing right into the back end of his car. He quickly dropped Marina like a rag doll and took off running. That must have shaken her enough to wake her up.

I saw Terrell run towards the second car as I ran in DJ's direction. I tackled his ass and started slugging him as hard as I could.

I just kept punching and punching until I heard a deep voice say "That's enough." I turned around to see Amon and another guy standing behind me. I looked past them to see Marina coming towards me with Cheryl and Terrell in tow. I got up so I could go to my woman. I could care less about DJ now that Amon was there. I knew he'd take care of him but how he got there was a mystery to me.

I embraced the love of my life and laid a kiss on her so deep that she needed to catch her breath afterwards. I checked her out and repeatedly asked her over and over again if she was ok. She assured me she was. I stood there holding Marina in my arms when Cheryl broke the ice.

"Y'all are wondering how Amon got here right? Well once I found my keys I ran back over to the car and almost tripped on something. I realized that it was Marina's phone. After overhearing bits and pieces of what happened with Marina and Colay kidnapping her, I figured out that this Amon dude must be somebody big. I called him and he thought I was Marina. I explained to him what happened and he said he was on the way."

"But how did he get here so fast?"

"Well babe that was my doing. I told you I had a plan but you wouldn't listen to me. I hit Amon up when Cheryl went to get the car so I could have some privacy. He told me he'd come down to help me but to go ahead with whatever you had prearranged. How Cheryl got him here though was all on her."

I stood there beaming at my woman. She was a sneaky little thing but I loved her nonetheless. It was time to go get our kids and live happily. Amon let us know that he'd be in contact with us within the next few days and with that we were on our way back to Fayetteville. I just wanted a hot shower and a good night's sleep.

The next afternoon I woke up refreshed as ever. I noticed that Marina wasn't in the bed next to me. I guessed that she was in the kids' room a few floors down. I wasn't worried now that all of our problems were gone. I took a quick shower and threw something on before heading downstairs to be with my family. I had something planned for the day and I would need the little ones to help me out.

I walked into the kids' room to see everybody there. I was in love with the sight in front of me. Marina was a great woman and mother. My mama was a great pillar of strength. My brothers always had my back. There was definitely a lot of love in that room. I hushed everybody for a second so I could get the kids' attention.

"So since your mom and I have been so busy lately, I've decided to take you all out to Golden Corral then over to the mall for some shopping. What do y'all think?"

The kids started going haywire and talking at once. All I heard was Build-A-Bear Workshop, The Disney Store and food. I was cool with that. Marina helped me get them all together and down to the car. After she helped me buckle everybody in she started to climb her tail into the passenger seat when I stopped her.

"Sorry babes. This trip is only for me and the kids I got you though. I set up a spa day for you, Cheryl and mom at The Renaissance in Eutaw Shopping Center next to the roller skating rink. Enjoy your day babe and I'll see you later."

She stood there with the pouty face until I told her about the spa. Then she was all smiles and gave me the biggest kiss ever. I watched her bounce away all happy. I drove off with the kids headed towards Cross Creek Mall. They were gonna help me find their mama a ring.

Marina

Lucky for my ass that I had that last minute backup plan. If it wasn't for that, things may have turned out for the worst. When I called Amon, he seemed so nonchalant. That made me think he was going to stand down but naw, he came through like a fucking champ. I had to give it to him, his timing was impeccable.

That was the first time in a while that I had slept so peacefully and what better place to be besides in the arms of the one who loved me. I couldn't ask for much more.

My slumber only lasted until sunrise. No matter how hard I tried to go back to sleep, I couldn't. I was too damn anxious to see my kids and kiss all over them.

Easing out of the bed quietly, I slid on my sweats and T-shirt and went downstairs. Of course they were all already up. They paid me no mind. They were too damn busy jumping all over the place. It warmed my heart to see them so happy.

Picking up the hotel phone, I dialed Cheryl and Terrell's suite to see what they were doing. I was hungry and was ready to get my grub on. I had been doing that a lot lately.

"What's up Marina? I was just about to call you."

"Good Morning Cheryl. What cha guys doin'?"

"We just got dressed and was about to go get something to eat. Where are you?"

"I'm in the kid's room. Y'all come over here first."

They came right over and Timothy wasn't too far behind them. I thought he was coming to find me. Shit, he came for the kids, but he sure didn't leave me out. He sent all of us ladies to the spa! I had never been before so my ass was geeked!

We were ready and out the door within the hour and I still hadn't eaten. My stomach was turning and I started feeling sick. I hurried to grab a soda on the way to calm it down but that only made me hungrier.

"Are you okay Marina?" Cheryl asked me once Timothy's mother got out of earshot.

"Yeah girl, I'm just feeling a little woozy," I admitted as I began to sweat profusely.

Helping me take a seat while we were waiting to go to the back, Cheryl quickly got me a cold towel and placed it on my forehead. It cooled my body down quickly and I was beginning to feel a little better. I sat there with Timothy's mother while Cheryl ran off again and came right back.

"Here's some crackers and some cheese," Cheryl offered holding up a tray of snacks as if she worked there.

I didn't even question where she got it from. I just indulged until I was satisfied. Then it was time to get our royal treatment which took all damn day. For some reason I couldn't enjoy it fully.

Once we left, I could have sworn I saw a car following us. I didn't want to alert Cheryl or Timothy's mother, so I chilled until I knew for sure.

"Damn, I swear that looked like DJ," I thought silently as my heart raced with fear.

The dark sedan breezed by me so fast I couldn't be sure. I had to call Amon and make sure shit was taken care of. I had to be sure.

Opting to get something to eat before heading back to the hotel, we swung by a burger joint. I was still feeling on edge and Cheryl quickly peeped it out and called me on it. Not wanting to hold it in, I motioned her to meet me in the bathroom. Timothy's mother had just gotten her food, so I knew she wasn't going to try to question or follow us.

Stepping into the handicapped stall, I began to hold my nose at the horrible odor. The smell was similar to that of a pot of greens that had been sitting out overnight. The shit was not cool. I began to gasp and choke then suddenly I let loose a gang of 'Earl' in the toilet.

"Damn Marina! You coulda warned a bitch!" Cheryl shouted as she grabbed some tissue to help wipe my mouth. "What the fuck is goin' on with you?"

I didn't know what the fuck to tell her so I chalked it up to my nerves being wrecked. She agreed once I told her who I thought I saw on the road when we were on our way to the restaurant.

After cleaning myself up and freshening my mouth with a swig of mouthwash I had in my handbag, Cheryl suggested I call Amon and double check. When I did, I got a message saying the number was disconnected. I tried my best not to panic. Not only was I unsure about DJ being dead, I also worried about the rest of our payment.

"He probably disposed of that cell once the shit was over Marina. Don't worry about that shit. Amon told you that he would get with you in a couple of days. At least give the man that."

Cheryl was right, but it wasn't enough to ease my mind about the situation with DJ. I needed to know as soon as possible if he was maggot food. I needed to know that shit like yesterday.

We hurried to get back out to join Timothy's mother and to enjoy our meal. She didn't say a word, but hell she was always quiet. She didn't talk unless it was necessary. She sat back and observed, that's why she was the smartest woman I knew. That woman never missed a beat. Even though she never mentioned a word about anything that was going on, she knew. She stayed on top of shit. I could tell by her gestures and emotions. Over that short period of time knowing her, I was able to read her. We definitely had a different kind of connection. That was up until that day.

When we got back in the car, she began to tell me about where my relationship with her son was headed. She surprised even me.

"Marina I just want to thank you for coming into my son's life when you did. You not only won his heart, you made him a better man. Y'all may have had to go through some mess, but that's just the thing to make your bond untouchable. You are a very special woman."

Speechless is just what I was. My tears began to stream and I let them. I couldn't even tell her how I was feeling. I didn't have to. She just patted my shoulder and told me she loved me. She told me that her son and I had an amazing future ahead of us. I believed her.

When we made it back to the hotel, Timothy and the kids were still gone. His mother went to the suite to wait for them. Cheryl went to meet Terrell who was blowing up her cell, so I was left all alone. I took that time to go to my room and wait on my man. I was all fresh and looking good. I couldn't wait for him to see me. It had been a minute since I fixed myself up.

Over an hour passed and he still wasn't back. I tried my best not to panic about the chance of DJ being alive, but I chose not to let that ruin my day. I closed my eyes and quickly dozed off.

"Marina, baby wake up!" Timothy requested along with shaking my body.

All the fucking motion sent my tummy in an uproar and next thing I knew I was 'letting loose' all over the bed and floor. I couldn't control it.

Timothy rushed in the bathroom and got me some wet washcloths. He assisted me out of the bed and onto the sofa in the living room area of the suite. I didn't know what had come over me. I was letting my worrying get the best of me.

We called room service and had someone clean up the mess. They moved us to the room next door so that we wouldn't have to be disturbed while they took care of it.

By the time we got our things in the new suite, my stomach was settled, but Timothy wasn't. He just sat there looking at me with a big ass grin on his face. That was one time I couldn't read him, so I stayed quiet and waited for him to speak first.

"Are you okay baby?"

"I think so. Why ya ask me like that?"

"Marina is there something you want to tell me?"

My mind shifted to what I thought I saw earlier. I figured Cheryl must have told him so I just spilled my guts to avoid a confrontation. When I finished, Timothy looked dumbfounded. I knew then that was not what he expected me to reveal.

"Did you call Amon?"

"Yes and his number was disconnected."

"Are you fuckin' kiddin' me right the fuck now?"

Timothy got on his cell and dialed his brother Terrell. He came right over to the room with Cheryl and the kids in tow.

"Well damn, I thought this was going to be a special day." Terrell blurted out.

When I looked at Timothy in confusion, he was waving his brother off and telling him to hush. Then he diverted everyone's attention to the matter at hand, DJ.

I wasn't sure what everybody was hiding from me, but I was about to get to the bottom of shit. If there was something I needed to know, folks better had start speaking the fuck up.

As my anger level rose, Timothy swiftly calmed me with a kiss and told me to take it easy. He pulled me close into a tight embrace. That's when I felt something bulky in his front pocket. I backed up from him and questioned it.

Timothy hesitated and then told me to hold on while he and Terrell contacted Tina to find out what they could. Her and Amon were holding a conversation before we left the house, so he thought she might know how to get in touch with him.

Yeah, I loved how he didn't answer my question about the contents in his pocket, but I was determined to find out...

Timothy

   While the grownups discussed things, the kids ran off to play in the living area of the suit. I was waiting patiently for Terrell to get off the line with Tina. Once he did, he confirmed that DJ was no longer a threat. Apparently Amon needed a chick like her on his team so he offered her a job. I wasn't mad at her for that and now maybe with her gone, Cheryl wouldn't trip on my brother anymore. Now it was time for me to get back to what I was trying to do.

   When we went back into the living room Marina was nowhere to be found. I was confused. How the hell did she disappear that fast? I started to ask Cheryl where my woman was at but then I heard the toilet flush. Marina appeared shortly thereafter. I smiled at the thought of what I was about to do.

   I looked around the room at all the smiling faces. My gaze stopped on Marina and I couldn't stop smiling. She was looking at me strangely so I decided to speak.

"Babe you have made me the happiest man ever. I love you with everything I got in me. I wanted to know if you would do me the honor of being my wife. Will you marry me?"

I dropped down to one knee as I pulled the ring box out of my pocket. I opened it so I could show her the shiny piece of 'Bling'. It was a beautiful 2-carat princess cut sapphire and diamond engagement ring. I waited for my queen to give me an answer.

"Yes! Yes baby I'll marry you!"

I slipped the ring on her finger as I jumped up to embrace her. She was crying and hugging me so tight but I wouldn't have it any other way. There was no way this day, this moment, could get any better. The kids ran to get her the flowers I bought her earlier and Cheryl and Terrell handed her a card that I also bought. I watched as she read the card.

My Queen, My Love, My Everything,
Ever since you came into my life I have become a better man. Everything about you makes me want to be better and do better. There's nothing more I want in this life than to be with you forever. Here's to a lifetime of love, happiness and forever being my queen. I love you babe.
Your King,
Timothy

Out of the card fell a slip of paper. It was given to me earlier today by our realtor who I just so happened to see in the mall. I watched as she read it, not once but twice. She started jumping up and down again. That time she yelled too. I was happy to see her happy like that. Cheryl rushed over to Marina to see what all the fuss was about. Soon she was jumping and hollering too. I asked Marina to tell everybody what was going on. We all listened as she read from the paper out loud.

To whom it may concern:

The property at 533 Winding Rd, Sanford, NC 27332 has been paid in full in the amount of $132,467.00 and now belongs to a Miss Marina Labrador. The property is co-owned by her children as well. This dwelling was bought as a gift by a Mr. Amon Thomas.

Janice Tomlinson

RE/MAX Real Estate Services

The whole room cheered as Marina rushed over to me. She was happy so I was happy. For the rest of my life I planned on making her stay just like this. I pulled Marina into me and laid a deep passionate kiss on her. There was a chorus of "ewww" as we did so. I laughed about it and so did she. I swear that was the happiest day of my life.

"Babe did I tell you how happy you've made me?"

"No babe tell me."

"Not only did you accept me and my children as a packaged deal but you love all of us unconditionally. I love you so much for that."

"I love you too babe and nothing could make me happier right now."

"Wanna bet?"

Marina had a sly smiled spread across her face. I cocked my head to the side and looked at her like I was seeing her for the first time. I couldn't figure out what she was about to tell me but whatever it was I wasn't worried. I pulled her in for another kiss before I asked my next question.

"So what could you possibly do to make me happier than I already am?

"How about make you a daddy?"

"A baby! Really?"

"Yes!"

She pulled out a small rectangular pregnancy test from her back pants pocket. I looked at the two bright pink lines that showed a positive pregnancy test. That was the best news Marina had ever given me besides the time she told me she loved me. I wanted to marry her now more than ever.

Epilogue

TWO MONTHS LATER.......

Even though I didn't get to marry Marina before we moved into our new house, I still made it happen. We were all moved in before her first OB/GYN appointment. When we went to the doctor's appointment we found out that she was nine weeks along. I was excited to become a father but it still wouldn't take away from my other kids.

Yeah I said my other kids because I felt as though they were my own. Now with Colay gone, I gladly stepped up to play that role to them. I wanted to show the girls how a man was supposed to love a woman and I wanted to show the boys how they're supposed to love a woman. Our life was good.

We planned a small intimate wedding ceremony at my mother's church where I grew up at with the money that Amon had delivered to us. As I watched my beautiful, glowing, pregnant bride walk down the aisle escorted by both of her brothers, I couldn't help but feel honored. All the people in the world and she chose me. Soft music played in the background. It was the chorus to my baby's favorite song.....

Who wants that perfect love story anyway, anyway......

Cliché, cliché, cliché, cliché

Who wants that hero love that saves the day, anyway

Cliché, cliché, cliché, cliché

Made in the USA
Middletown, DE
07 June 2015